I0537665

On Angel Wings
A Love's Pure Light Novella
Janine Rosche

LOVE WANDER READ
Publications

Love Wander Read Publications

Also By Janine Rosche

With Every Memory
The Road Before Us (May 2024)

<u>The Madison River Romance Series</u>
Mistletoe Menagerie
This Wandering Heart
Wildflower Road
Glory Falls

<u>The Whisper Canyon Series</u>
Aspen Crossroads

<u>Short Stories, Novellas, and Novelettes</u>
Dreams in Toyland
The Last First Kiss
Courting Mr. Collins
The Other Mr. Wickham (May 2024)

Dedicated to those who served during the Second World War, both on the home front and abroad, especially the Angels of Bataan and Corregidor, 2nd LT. George F. Mitchell, Jr., of the 386th division of the US Army Air Corps, and Corporal Robert W. Rosche Sr., of the 309 Troop Carrier group of the US Army Air Corps.

And suddenly there was with the angel a multitude of the heavenly host praising God, and saying, "Glory to God in the highest, and on earth peace, good will toward men."

Luke 2:13-14

Chapter One

Hope Hill, Missouri
Thanksgiving Day, 1945

E ver since Elodie Wise was a little girl, she'd been told she carried a light inside her soul that even the darkest night could not snuff out. The only problem? When she wanted—or rather needed—to hide, she never could. That didn't keep her from trying, of course.

With hardly any sound, she crept backward, keeping her weight on her hands and heels until she'd settled into the blackest space she could find. Hugging her knees to her chest, she waited for the threat to fade away. Hinges squeaked, scaling up, then down, and a frigid breeze slithered through the darkness. It found her, coiling around her legs. While the chill snaked into the marrow of her bones, she remained still as the dead.

Something scurried nearby. Something big. Her heart drummed the rhythm of "Chattanooga Choo Choo" against her chest. Just as she'd done countless times before, she sang the words of Psalm Twenty-Seven in her head, pairing the words to the beat.

The Lord is my light
and my salvation;
who-oom shall I fear?
the Lord is the strength of my life...

And, like always, a nonsensical peace washed over her so completely that the hot breath against her neck hardly frightened her at all.

"I don't think she saw us." Benjamin. His whisper soothed away her remaining jitters. "We should be safe here."

"I'm not sure. She's relentless." Elodie rocked to the side, nudging her old friend.

On the other side of the cardboard box barricade, the door to the garage protested being opened again. Benjamin pulled Elodie against him, blanketing her back, shoulder, and arm with velvety warmth. A sharp contrast to the icy concrete below.

With a click, the single bulb attached to the ceiling flooded the space with light. "Elodie Lila Wise, you'll catch your death of cold out here." Her mother's voice carried over the maze of stacked boxes that held her family's memorabilia, old playthings, and Christmas decorations. "I'm getting the pies out, and I made all your favorites. Elodie?"

With a glance over her shoulder, she met Benjamin's mischievous gaze.

He raised a finger to his lips.

Elodie clapped her hand to her mouth, trapping her chuckle inside.

"Oh, gracious. Ben, when you two are done playing hide-and-seek, bring Elodie inside, please."

"Yes, ma'am." The rich depth of his voice made one thing clear. They were no longer kids hiding from chores. After the door shut, Benjamin circled Elodie's wrist with his thumb and middle finger. "Sweetheart," he said, in his best impression of her mother, "come inside and let me fatten you up. I've added extra lard to the chocolate pie. I shall spoon-feed it to you while your father smothers you with hugs." His voice cracked into laughter.

"It feels silly the way they baby me. But I can't say I blame them. I've only gained back half of what I lost over there."

"Give it time. It took, what? Three years to lose that weight? You'll get there. Even so, war heroes deserve some good pumpkin pie."

"Like you?"

"Oh yeah. I'm a real hero. All I did was babysit Mister America, Clyde Irving." The sarcasm was as thick as her mother's mashed potatoes. "I was a joke, and you know it."

"Benjamin Gabriel, you were not, and never could be a joke. You were the best soldier the army had. Why else would they assign you the job of keeping the most famous actor in Hollywood from getting killed?"

"Spare me, will you? It was nothing more than a parade of destruction through Europe. One that went past all the battles our real soldiers fought days before." Shame weighed on his brow.

Was there anything she could say to help him the way he'd always helped her? "You were a real soldier. I know you don't believe me, but other than MacArthur, I think you had the most important job of all. If something had happened to Clyde Irving, the whole country might have lost hope."

"Yeah, yeah."

She placed a hand on his face and offered him her best smile. "It kept us nurses going, I can tell you that much. The girls would fawn all over him. 'Clyde's going to set us free. Clyde's fighting the Nazis. Clyde's marching on Tokyo.' And every time, I'd say, 'If he is, it's because of my Benjamin.'"

His eyes darted across the floor, then settled on her face. "You told them about me?"

"All the time." Her words unleashed a smile that lit up his face. "I'd tell them that you're the bravest man in the whole world—the brother I'd always wanted."

He blinked. His lips fell, then twisted into a smirk. "Why are you out here again? I mean, other than avoiding your mother's attempts to spit-shine your cheeks—which, by the way, are a little dirty." He pretended to spit on his thumb and reached for her face.

Intercepting him, she grabbed his forearm. He'd gotten so strong. And handsome. Of course, he'd always been that. She was the one who, as Mama said, had to grow into her beauty. By that time, she'd joined the Army Nurse Corps and took her first assignment at Manila's Sternberg Hospital in the Philippines six weeks before the attack on Pearl Harbor. Not long after, she and others were taken captive and sent to Santo Tomas, a university-turned-internment camp where beauty counted for nothing.

"I started remembering where I was this time last year. Just needed a few minutes." She wished she could blame the cold, dry air in the garage for the constricting of her throat. Her left hand quaked—something that might embarrass her around anyone but Benjamin. Straightening her fingers into rigid spokes, she turned her palm up.

Benjamin's hand slid across until it aligned with hers, his fingertips extending past hers slightly. After ten seconds or so, her trembling eased.

"Since Thanksgiving was a wash, I'd like to start thinking about Christmas. Perhaps I'll be better by then." She needed something to focus on, other than the memories of war. Maybe then she could begin to truly live again. Accept the blessings God had placed right in front of her.

"Don't push yourself too hard, El." He wrapped his fingers around hers.

As a nurse, most of the hands she'd held were cold, frail, and waning of life. But Benjamin's hand was warm and strong. She hoped he didn't mind holding her hand a bit longer.

He didn't seem to. In fact, he held on tighter as they stood.

"Benjamin, will you help me find something? It's in one of these boxes labeled 'Christmas.'"

He was only a few inches taller than her. But what he lacked in height, he made up for in muscle, charisma, and a devout faith that had helped Elodie endure, even when half the world separated them. How he hadn't married already, she didn't understand. Any girl would love to have Benjamin gaze at her the way he did at Elodie now. Too bad she wasn't *any girl*. Not after what she'd been through.

Pressing his back against the wood, Benjamin held the door open for Elodie. With her arms cradling the wooden box, she had to turn sideways to fit through the frame. Her body brushed his, her hair wisping his nose. Every nerve in his body woke with a jolt.

"Now, Benjamin, I know you aren't making our little Sunshine carry that for you." Mr. Wise rushed to Elodie, but she shook her head.

Kneeling, she lowered the box to the carpet in the family room.

"I tried, sir, but she didn't trust me not to break it." Benjamin stayed close to Elodie. She breathed hard, the strain making her body waver slightly. He placed a hand under her elbow and guided her into a seated position, hoping her father hadn't seen. If her parents treated her any more like a porcelain doll, they'd hook her on a stand and place her on the highest shelf.

Mr. Wise had seen his share of combat during the Great War, and he and Mrs. Wise had fully supported Elodie's decision to join the Army Nurse Corps. But having her captured and held for three years had taken its toll on all of them.

"She says my mitts are too thick for handling this nativity set," Ben said.

"Did she bring up that broken angel again?" Mr. Wise reclaimed his spot in his leather chair. "At least it wasn't one of the heirloom figures or the wise men I carved for her mother. I think Stella bought that angel at Woolworth's for a dime the year Rhoda was born."

"Precisely. And it wasn't my fault Elodie has butterfingers. My throw was perfect. She was the one who dropped it."

Elodie slugged his arm. So much for that waning strength.

"Hey, bruiser, be nice." He deserved it, though. She'd cried and cried when that ill-fated angel fell and broke in two. His penalty was seeing her front door shut in his face every day for two weeks. They'd only been ten the Christmas of 1931, but he'd vowed never to make her cry again.

She feigned a hateful glare. "Still, you knew that was my favorite piece, you big lug."

"That's why I figured you'd catch it."

Her mother appeared, wiping her hands on her worn, checked apron. "The whipped cream is finished. Everyone to the table. Elodie, I got you a piece of chocolate pie and a piece of pumpkin pie, in case you're still hungry after one."

Mr. Wise met his wife in the doorway. He kissed her forehead and followed her lead into the kitchen.

Elodie met Benjamin's gaze. "That's my mother—sticking it to Japan and Germany, one dollop of whipped cream at a time."

At the table, Benjamin sat sandwiched between Elodie's two younger sisters. Although they shared their mother's golden hair and their father's light blue eyes, Charlie was Elodie's opposite in almost every way. He'd never once seen her wear a dress. And if anyone other than her family called her Charlotte, they'd be sure to get a fat lip. Ever since the war began, she'd been working for Heroes of Hope Hill, organizing support for the war effort on the home front.

The youngest of the Wise girls, on the other hand, idolized Elodie. Rhoda, the eighteen-year-old, dressed and acted just like her, with one glaring exception. Rhoda did not see Benjamin as a brother. Not one little bit.

Benjamin lifted Rhoda's hand off his knee and placed it on her own, shooting her a warning look in the process.

Elodie, sitting on his other side, smiled. Of course, she found Rhoda's crush humorous. Last week, she'd even encouraged him to take Rhoda out on a date. When he'd refused, she seemed puzzled. Yes, Elodie had been through a trauma in that internment camp, but had it made her utterly blind to his love for her? Driving his fork into the pumpkin pie, he prepared to eat his feelings, slathered with whipped cream.

"Benjamin, thank you for spending Thanksgiving with us," Mrs. Wise said.

"It's my pleasure, ma'am. Without you all, I'd be alone today, cooking for myself. And I'm not sure pumpkin pie comes in a can." He flashed them a grin of appreciation. After all, he loved them as much as he'd loved his own family. "My parents would thank you for taking me in."

"It can't be easy. Coming home to a world so different," Charlie said. She rested her elbows on the table, steepling her fingers. "It's all a mess. You know, I saw June Everhart at work the other day. Her kids asked if their daddy's going to be okay. He's struggling to cope with home life after returning from Europe."

"Charlie, please." Mrs. Wise's tone might have been enough to flatten the whipped cream if it wasn't already heavy with the heaps of sugar she'd added. Even the smallest task, she seemed to perform with her eldest daughter in mind.

Elodie poked at her pie but hadn't yet scooped a bite.

"Mama, we can't keep pretending all is fine around us. Of all people, Elodie knows that."

"That doesn't mean we should talk about it around the Thanksgiving table. Tomorrow, we will discuss how our family can help, but not right now." She smoothed her hair behind her ear.

"How can we help people if no one is willing to talk about what everyone is facing? In our county, there are one hundred and thirty-two empty seats at the table today. We have three people other than Elodie who are recovering from being prisoners of—"

"Charlie, we'll discuss this later," Mr. Wise said, a stern edge to his voice, which Benjamin knew from a childhood playing in this home, would only fuel the fire in Charlie's rebel soul.

As the argument over what constituted pleasant holiday table talk dragged on, Elodie straightened her hand. She flattened it on the table next to her plate. Her eyes met Benjamin's.

He put his fork down and, likewise, pressed his hand against the linen tablecloth, holding her gaze. He'd stay like this forever if she needed him to.

"I'd like to help." Elodie's voice was so low it burrowed beneath the plates and napkins.

No one heard her except him. Unacceptable.

Benjamin pounded his hand on the table.

The whole family stilled.

"Elodie has something to say."

She gave him a nod, then looked each person in the eye, one after the other. "Ever since returning home, I've been wracking my brain to find some way to help others affected by the war—"

"You've done enough to help—"

"Mama, please. They didn't break me. I can do more." As she spoke, her hand relaxed, her fingers slowly curling. "Charlie, if I could raise money somehow for Heroes of Hope Hill, are there services you can provide to families like the Everharts?"

Charlie's eyes popped open. Her lips moved before any words came out. "Yes! We can provide counseling, loans, gifts, scholarships, if we had the money."

Elodie placed a bite of chocolate pie in her mouth and then dabbed her napkin where the two most perfect lips in the world came together. "I'll think of something." She pushed back her chair, stood, then kissed her mother's cheek. "Great pie, Mama." Elodie disappeared into the family room.

Mrs. Wise began to rise, but Mr. Wise's hand on her arm settled her back into the chair. He looked at Benjamin. "Stella, let's let Ben check on her."

"Yes, sir." Ben waved off Rhoda's hand, which, like an annoying mosquito, touched the nape of his neck. As he rounded the doorframe, he found Elodie unpacking the nativity set. Carefully, she unrolled each figurine from the newspaper and placed it in front of the wooden crèche. She flattened the newsprint and pointed to the headline of an article dated just after Christmas last year.

"'Local Man Killed in Belgium,'" she read. "'Mrs. Frank Dover received news that her husband, an infantryman, was killed earlier this month while defending the port of Antwerp. He is survived by his wife, his parents Joyce and Elmer Dover of Park Street, and his two-year-old son, Frank Jr.'" Her fingernail marked an invisible line beneath the child's name. "Benjamin, if I can come up with an idea for a fundraiser to help the soldiers and their families, would you help me plan it?"

"You know I will." He unwrapped Joseph, handling the figure like a precious jewel. If he broke another piece, she'd never forgive him. Placing it beneath the roof of the crèche right next to Mary's kneeling form, he sang along to the song playing on the radio—"Chattanooga Choo Choo." Was she also thinking of the night they danced to that song?

"We could have a dance— a Christmas one. We could invite the families, but also people with deep pockets." Her words prattled faster with every detail about food, decorations, and possible locations. As she spoke, her spine lengthened. "With all the hoopla about the 'Battling Belles of Bataan,' maybe I could give a speech or show that star—"

"*That star*? You mean the Bronze Star?" He laughed at her near-constant humility.

"Yes, that one." Color tinged her cheeks. She was more alive than he'd seen her since she returned. "I could use my celebrity for good. Turn the darkness into light."

She leaned toward him in her excitement— almost close enough to kiss. Her nearness was entrancing.

"I wouldn't expect anything else from my girl." His thumb grazed her cheek. "I'm completely at your service, El. Anything you want, I'll get it for you. Just have to promise me one thing."

"What's that?"

"A dance," he said.

She smiled. "You got it."

His fingertips trailed down her jaw, settling on the side of her neck. Her skin was smooth as glass. Her eyes, as soothing as the French sky when his feet were surrounded by bloodstained rubble. All those wasted years he'd spent during the war, protecting one man on a propaganda campaign when he could have been doing more for his country, for his brothers-in-arms, for the interned people like Elodie. This was what kept him going. That one day, he might dance with her again. And maybe kiss her the way he should have before the war.

"Benjamin." His name on her breath filled him with courage he'd lacked back in '41. He moved toward Elodie, and her eyes grew wide. "Do you think you could get Clyde Irving to make an appearance?"

Chapter Two

"**Y**ou're a tough one to get a hold of, Clyde." Ben relaxed his grip on the telephone's handset. If his wartime pal hadn't answered this time, Ben was going to hop on the next bus to Los Angeles and track him down.

"If I weren't, everyone would get a piece of me. You know that." Clyde's movie star voice slid over the line smoother than hydraulic oil. However, Clyde Irving wasn't one to shy away from fans, cameras, or a good press opportunity. Over the years they'd spent together, Ben had seen the way Clyde offered pieces of himself to every passerby. "How are you, Benny? It's been too long. Have you reconsidered my offer to come out to Hollywood to be my assistant? There's a whole lot of pretty girls out here who'd love to meet an All-American kid like you."

Kid. Clyde was only five years older than Ben, although he acted younger than Rhoda. That didn't stop him from offering his wisdom. And Clyde's favorite subject to lend advice about? Women.

"Nah. I'm calling about something else."

"Oh, that's right. You're back home with that pretty gal pal of yours. Goldilocks."

"Elodie."

"Goldilocks. Elodie. One and the same. Let me guess. You came back, dropped down on one knee, and now you've got the house, the wife, and the baby on the way?"

"Not exactly." Ben hadn't hidden his adoration for Elodie from Clyde. They'd become friends of sorts, in the dark of night when the cameras shut off, and they were just two soldiers in a foreign land dredged with the muck of war. And yeah, Ben had talked a big game about all that he planned to do when he saw Elodie again. It would involve just what Clyde had mentioned.

But the Elodie that Ben had parted from before the war had returned with a shadow lurking behind her. They all had. And the cottage with a front porch and a big oak tree needed to be put on hold. Not that she'd changed entirely. She was still Ben's childhood chum, but she needed to find her place again. Maybe this fundraiser would help.

"My manager wants me to settle down. Can you believe that? Clyde Irving settle down with just one woman? Foolishness. But he says it would be good for my image."

Just last week, Clyde had been spotted out with yet another young starlet. This one barely eighteen. The two were caught canoodling late into the night outside a Hollywood bar. While middle America didn't love his gallivanting ways, they were still fascinated by his celebrity. And he'd bring in the big bucks for Elodie's cause.

"I have another idea for how you can rebuild your image," Ben said. "Elodie is hosting a fundraising ball on December 23. The money will go to helping veterans adjust to their lives at home as well as families whose soldiers won't come home at all. It's something she's passionate about and—"

"You're passionate about her."

Ben said nothing.

"You need me to make an appearance? Over Christmas?"

Clyde didn't have family. It was a topic they'd bonded over. But whereas Ben lost his father in '37 and his mother one year later, Clyde had been orphaned before he reached the age of ten. Another difference? Clyde liked to brag that he preferred to spend his holidays with a bottle of liquor. It'd be good for him to experience a Christmas in Hope Hill.

"It's a nice little place. Not the worst spot to celebrate Christ's birth."

Clyde scoffed. "Will I get to meet Elodie? The way you rattle on and on about the girl, I wonder if she exists at all. She might be one of those angels that book of yours speaks of."

"You mean the Bible?" Ben laughed. "You should pick one up. It won't burn your fingertips if you touch it."

"And read a list of all my sins? No, thank you," Clyde said. "I'll have to clear my schedule, but I can make that happen. We both know I owe you one."

Yes. Ben knew that all too well.

Judy Garland's voice spilled through the Chevrolet's radio. The toasty air kissed Elodie's face as she sat in the passenger seat next to Charlie. Through the windshield, the abandoned airplane hangar towered into the Missouri sky. Funny how the sight of an ugly steel building could summon sprinkles of joy. But there was a time not so long ago when Elodie, surrounded by concrete walls, shacks, the jungle, and fencing, wondered if she'd ever see anything like this again. Such a silly thought. She wouldn't share that with her sister. Now Ben? She could share that with Benjamin. He'd never think her silly.

She craned her neck to see if his old truck was in sight. Not yet. His shift as a mechanic on base only ended fifteen minutes ago. But soon, she'd hear that old rumbling engine—a sound that, for some reason, was good for more than mere sprinkles of joy. Instead, she felt a blizzard of it whenever Benjamin was near. It swirled around her, lifting her hair off her neck, and blanketing her with reminders of all the good that the war hadn't stolen.

"This song. . ." Charlie scooched across the bench seat, then latched onto the crook of Elodie's arm, hugging her close. "When I saw *Meet Me in St. Louis* last year in the theater, and she sang this song, I threw my box of popcorn on the ground and ran out of the theater."

Ooh. Must have been serious. Charlie loved her popcorn. Even more, Charlie, a big proponent of rationing, hated wasting food of any kind.

"All those promises she made about *next year*? I didn't believe one word of it. That loved ones would all be gathered round the tree together. That our troubles would vanish. With you still captured? My faith truly faltered."

"Aww, Charlie."

"Luckily, Ben stopped me from causing too big of a scene out there on the street. While I was trying to find a way to climb up to the marquee—I was going to tear down every letter from the movie title so no one else would see it—he talked sense into me."

Elodie stared hard at the hangar doors. "You went to the movie with Benjamin?"

Judy finished her song, and the jingle of a local shop's advertisement began. Charlie didn't answer. Ben had returned from duty last November, almost three months before Elodie's liberation. Why should she be so concerned, anyway?

"Did Mama tell you? Three boys from town are scheduled to arrive at the train station on the twenty-first, including George Weston."

"The same George that Rhoda has been writing to?"

"The very one. He'll be home for Christmas. And the ball."

"Charlie, what if the fundraiser was also a homecoming for George and the other men on the transport? The crowd will love to see them. And they may give more when they see the heroes their money will be helping."

Charlie grinned. "That's a fine idea. I'll have Rhoda write George about it and make sure he's on board. What about Clyde Irving? Will he make an appearance?"

"No word yet. Benjamin promised me he'd make it happen, though."

"If he promised, then Clyde will be here. Ben's the reliable sort." Charlie sucked in a long, slow breath. A trick Elodie remembered Daddy had taught Charlie during childhood to force her to think through the words threatening to dart off her tongue. It didn't always work. "Hey, El. Do you plan to bring a date to the ball?"

"No. Why?"

"Have you thought much about dating, marriage, men in general?"

"Funny you should ask." Elodie brushed a stray hair off her forehead. She lifted her arm free of Charlie's hold, then worked to repin the tendrils at her crown. Difficult without a mirror, but if it looked a fright, only Charlie and Benjamin would see. And he didn't give a lick about what she looked like. "I always thought I'd be married by now. To a tall, strapping fella. With a kind face and a sophisticated style. Like Cary Grant or Jimmy Stewart."

"Clyde Irving?"

"Goodness. No. He's too handsome."

"Well, if you're opposed to handsome, I guess Ben is off the ballot."

Charlie found Benjamin attractive? Elodie rubbed a hand up the lapel of her coat, then back down again. She'd expected Rhoda to go after Benjamin. Rhoda loved any boy who paid her mind. But Charlie wasn't to be swayed by an easy smile or smooth line. Any man she chose would have to be intelligent, funny, driven, and yes, handsome. That was Benjamin in a nutshell.

And Charlie was smart, witty, and full of life. Why wouldn't Benjamin fall for her in return? He'd be good for Charlie. He could encourage her passions while also tempering her fiery ways. So why did her chest ache at the thought?

"I'm not so sure I'd be a good girlfriend or wife to anyone right now," Elodie said. "There's still too much muddling my head. I can't imagine taking in a picture show or going to a fair. To pretend the world is fine? Every day we're learning more and more about the atrocities of the past few years. You understand, don't you?"

"Of course I do. But wouldn't you love for a brave soldier to get the help he needs so he could go to the fair and to picture shows without the memories of war haunting him?"

Elodie nodded.

"That's why our work is so important, Sis. We're bringing light one way or another."

The chug of an engine approached from the road. Benjamin's truck pulled up beside them. And when his eyes met Elodie's, his crooked smile beamed. She gave a small wave in reply. Elodie's joy, while still present, had calmed a bit from the heavy talk. Ben's eyes shifted to Charlie's, and he nodded. Charlie winked. *Winked*. At her Benjamin.

No. That wasn't right. Benjamin was a friend to her whole family. Elodie didn't get to claim him. Again, her joy dipped. Why, though?

"I wonder who Benjamin will escort to the ball. Maybe he'll take a friend. That's allowed, you know." Charlie nudged Elodie—not as hard as she would have years ago. "Now, let's go see this place."

Inside the hangar, Ben could almost see the dance come to life as Elodie pointed out where the food and punch would be served and how the tables could be set up. He was glad for this project. Even moments ago, outside between their cars, darkness caped her eyes, just as it had so often since she'd returned home.

"We'll build the stage here, big enough for a full band." Elodie waved her arm toward the south end of the space, which currently held a stash of gasoline cans. She dipped her chin and spread her delicate hands out from her waist like she was smoothing sheets on a bed. "And this will be the dance floor."

An elbow dug into his ribs.

He pinned Charlie with a glare, but her eyes were full of challenge. The same elbow that had assaulted him now turned into a chicken wing that batted the back of his arm, nudging him forward. Ben refocused on Elodie.

She stood still, watching his exchange with her sister. Her expression had sobered. Why?

"It's the perfect place for a dance floor. Let's give it a try." He moved forward, taking her hand and easing her toward him.

"Wouldn't you rather dance with Charlie? She's much better than me." Elodie spun on her heels and walked toward the space she'd designated as an auction display.

Over his shoulder, Ben glanced at Charlie.

She shrugged. "El, I promised I'd stop at the market for Mama. Ben will have to drive you home."

"I thought you had all these ideas to share."

"I do. I'll tell you later, though. Mama wanted roast tonight, so I should get a move on. See you." Charlie scurried to the door before the confusion wrinkling Elodie's brow could fall to her lips.

Ben might have been miffed at Charlie's awkward exit if he wasn't so happy to have time with Elodie alone. Charlie was a fun kid sister-type, but after too much time with her, he was always ready for her metaphorical naptime. He joined Elodie but didn't try for the dance again. One rejection was enough for the day.

"I can build the stage if you want. Your father could help, I'm sure. I've got the hands for it, and the know-how." He held his hands up, only to notice how the oil from his job had stained his skin and lined his fingernails. Quickly, he dug them deep into his coat pockets.

Her gaze followed the movement, then bounced back up to his eyes. "What about me? I can help. I know how to use a hammer. And as I recall, you only got through geometry with my help. And French class too."

"So you thought."

"What does that mean?"

"Did you ever consider that the reason I let you help me with my homework was so you'd lean in close to me?"

Elodie blinked several times before she responded. "Why would you do that?"

"Because when you concentrate hard on something, you whisper real soft. It's cute." Ben rocked on his heels. He should stop there, but he didn't want to. He ached to show her his true feelings. He stepped toward her, pausing at her side to speak into her ear. "And you smell nice too." He moved past her, checking the wall. There was a draft coming in somewhere. It would be hard enough to keep this place warm for the dance without rogue breezes finding their way in. Plus, this kept his flushed face out of sight. He wasn't used to such forward flirtation with her. Flirtation that dared take them beyond friendship. Or, in her perception, beyond brother and sister.

"Ben, do you. . .?"

He turned to find her chewing her lip. That was no good. "Do I what?"

"Are you interested in Charlie?"

He nearly swallowed his tongue. Charlie? "Why on earth would you think that?"

Her blue eyes rounded beneath arched brows. "Because you two get along so well, and you share these moments. And last year, you saw *Meet Me in St. Louis* with her."

Ben might've bored a hole in the ceiling if he concentrated on it any harder. How much to say? "I asked her to see the movie with me because I needed to be near a friend. I'd just gotten back from Europe, and I wasn't doing well. Not at all. Frankly, neither was she. I went with her because she was the closest person to you that I could find. And I needed to be near someone who was just as worried about you as I was."

"I heard you followed her out of the theater when she got upset."

"Yeah. She needed to calm down." He rubbed the back of his neck, still remembering how tight those muscles had been as he'd fretted over Elodie's safety for more than three years. "Elodie, I don't know if I ever told you this, but I missed you like crazy during the war."

"Oh, Benjamin. I missed you too."

"I'm not interested in dating your sister." *I want to date you,* his heart begged his lips to say. But he needed to go slow with this.

She nodded but said no more. Perhaps he was mistaken, but relief appeared to wash over her. He'd never known her to be jealous of anything—not the neighbor girl's new bike, or her friend winning the homecoming queen title. But he might have finally found something Elodie wanted only for herself. The possibility, slim as it was, brought a smile to his face.

"This dance is going to be a great success. The soldiers will get a fantastic welcome back. It will be a grand celebration for the whole town. And you'll raise a ton of money that will help these heroes and families." Ben urged himself not to pause too long. Otherwise, Elodie would give him that same old lecture that he was a hero too. Not so. "Which brings me to the big news I wanted to share with you. I finally heard back from Clyde. He'll be here."

Elodie's brows shot higher than a cork on V-E Day. And the widest smile he'd seen in four years etched her face. Joy. Over Clyde. Once again, Ben's dream was overshadowed by his friend. When Elodie's bright blue eyes hazed, and the first tears spilled over her lashes, she threw herself at him. His arms needed no message from his brain to know what to do next. She fit so perfectly against him that he figured God designed him for the specific purpose of embracing her. Growing up, he'd always wanted to be taller than his five-foot-ten frame, but he'd grown to like only having a few inches on Elodie. He liked that, when they hugged, the slope of her slender neck aligned with the curve of his shoulder. It would make a kiss effortless if they ever got to that point.

"Thank you, Benjamin." Elodie's voice was small, and Ben wanted to take it and place it in his breast pocket to keep near his heart forever.

Chapter Three

"How's the planning coming? You aren't overdoing it, are you? You look tired." The concern on her mother's face stretched wider than Manila Bay.

"Mama, I'm fine."

"If it gets to be too much—"

"I'll walk away. But it's all coming together swell. The community has been dropping off strings of Christmas lights, tables, and chairs. We've even had all the lumber for the stage donated. Benjamin and I will start building it tomorrow after we get off work."

"You let him build that. If you want, you can hold the nails."

"Oh, Mama. . ."

Benjamin appeared at the back door, carrying two boxes. Elodie hurried to open the door for him. He passed by her, noting his thanks, then made his way to the family room. A few seconds later, he returned. "I think those were the ornaments and stockings. Just one more box. Are there more in the attic, Mrs. Wise?"

"No, dear. I think that's it."

"Okay, I'll be back in a jiffy." Benjamin flashed a grin at Elodie before disappearing out the back door that led to the garage.

"What a smile," her mother said.

"He's got a great one."

"I was talking about yours." Her mother dug her hands into the biscuit dough and began to combine the wet and dry ingredients. "Benjamin Gabriel will make a fine husband one day."

Elodie shook her head. At least her mother wasn't pushing her into marriage. Benjamin would have to deal with that himself. "Yes, he will. What a lucky girl she'll be. I'm going to look in the boxes, for old time's sake."

"You do that, sweetheart."

In the family room, Elodie unfolded the flaps of the first box marked *Ornaments*, finding its contents scarce. Where had all the colorful bulbs gone? Besides the heirloom nativity figurines, they'd been among her mother's prized holiday decorations. Every year, she'd add to the collection, even during the lean years before the war.

"Rhoda, where did all our ornaments go?" Her sister, who had been lying on her stomach and reading in front of the fireplace, didn't bother to look up.

"Mama pitched them."

"When?"

"After you left. No, after we joined the war, I think."

"Why on earth would she do that?"

"They were German glass, remember? She wouldn't let us hang those. No siree."

"What did you hang on the tree?"

Rhoda splayed her book flat on the ground, its front and back cover facing up to the ceiling. Then she rolled herself up to a seated position and sighed. "We didn't have one for that first year. In '42, there weren't men to chop them down, so the lots were empty. And we were too busy collecting materials for the war effort to do it ourselves. Not sure anyone was in much of a mood to celebrate Christmas anyway. Talk about crummy."

Elodie's thoughts trailed to her recent holidays behind fences topped with shards of glass. Even last Christmas Day, when the planes dropped flyers promising that liberation was near, it was hard to celebrate while the camp lost several to starvation every day. Thank the Lord that Rhoda didn't understand the full breadth of what others had endured. Still, Elodie forced herself to feel compassion for her little sister. "That must have been tough."

"We simply went to church and shared a meal. A small one with sausage disguised as turkey. Isn't that a hoot?"

"It sure is," Elodie said. Sacrifices were made on the home front as well. She mustn't forget that.

Benjamin rounded the corner with a large box propped on his shoulder. "I've got it."

"Thanks, Benny!" Rhoda popped up from the ground, then kissed him on his cheek. When she did, his eyes flickered to Elodie's, but she glanced away. Goodness. Her stomach twisted something awful. Like when she'd gone too long without food—a feeling she knew too well.

The box slid in front of her.

"'Visca,'" she read off the side of the box. "What is this?"

Rhoda pulled on what appeared to be branches. "Our tree. It's not very big. A tabletop display is all."

Elodie hid her grin with a hand. Even before she had time to form words, the box got yanked away, leaving artificial needles pinched between Rhoda's fingers.

Her mother heaved the box up into her arms. "This year, we'll get a real tree. Like that last Christmas we were all together. They have some down at the lot. A fir, perhaps. There's no need to bring that hideous thing back out."

"Mama, I like it." Rhoda flattened her hands against the ground. Her brows pinched together above the bridge of her button nose.

"We'll have an old-fashioned Christmas or none at all." Mama's tone was resolute. Then she was gone along with Rhoda's tree.

Across from Elodie, Rhoda sat back and crossed her arms. Her lips pursed. She shot a brief glare in Elodie's direction before swiveling her whole body toward the window where flurries fell. It wasn't fair. At only eighteen, she was still forming childhood memories. And Elodie's presence was unspooling them all.

Benjamin rubbed his hands together. "Rhoda, what do you say we head down to the tree lot and pick out a tree so grand it will flatten my tires?"

She perked up. "Just me and you?"

"And Elodie. If she wants to go."

Rhoda groaned.

Elodie inched closer to her sister. "Rhoda, I bet that little tree looks pretty all lit up with lights." She placed a hand on her sister's forearm, but Rhoda shrugged it off.

"Go have fun with your boyfriend already." Before Elodie could lift her jaw off the floor, Rhoda had jumped up and skirted out of the room.

"What was that about?" she asked Benjamin.

Red splotches crept up his neck. "I have no idea." His voice cracked on the last syllable. He cleared his throat and held his hand out to her. "Come on. Let's go get that tree."

Benjamin finished loading the tree Elodie had deemed perfect in the back of his truck. Sap glued two of his fingers together. He separated them, but the stickiness remained.

Elodie eyed him. "Did you get a sliver?" She took his hand in hers, only to drop it. Her soft intake of breath sent his nerves into a tizzy. "Ew, sap."

He laughed, prompting her to lay a playful slap on his arm.

"You could've warned me." She studied her fingers, then, with a smirk on her face, rubbed her hand down his coat, shoulder to ribs. Her touch was positively electric, like one caress on this tree could set it aglow, no lights required.

Lord, let her feel this too. Not that I deserve her. No one could. She's the closest thing to an angel I've ever seen.

Slowly, she withdrew her hand. Her crooked smile went flat as she raised her eyes to his.

"You practice your profession faithfully. Isn't that what that nursing pledge says? The one you recited at your graduation. You can't help but jump in, whether it's a sliver or something worse." He reached down into a pile of shoveled snow, grabbing a handful, then rubbed it between his palms. Once it had melted, he took Elodie's hand, and, not knowing the exact spot the sap had touched, methodically rubbed his thumb in circles over her palm. When she didn't recoil her hand, he continued, stroking his thumb down each of her fingers, knuckle to perfectly manicured nail. Her skin was so fair and unblemished compared to his knicked-up and stained hands. Embarrassment gnawed at him, and he released his hold on her.

"Thank you. I think you cleaned it off." Her voice was softer than usual, and she hadn't backed away.

"I should get you home."

"Or we could make a night of it." A touch of mischief danced across her face.

"Won't your mother worry?"

"Not if I'm with you," she said. "After all, the government trusted you to keep our country's most prized celebrity safe in a war. She knows there's no safer place for me than by your side." After she looped her arm around his, all other arguments fled.

A half hour later, they walked beneath colored bulbs that had been strung streetlight to streetlight. Main Street in Hope Hill was bustling on this Saturday night with shoppers eager to stuff presents beneath their trees Christmas morning. Lines of people waited outside the cinema to see *The Bells of St. Mary's*. Although he wouldn't mind taking in a flick and maybe placing his arm around her if she gave off the right signals, Elodie wanted to see the window displays. With the way she hugged his arm every time a chilly breeze passed between alleyways, that was just fine by him. And since it was cold, she remained quite close.

They paused a long while to take in a department store's window display. Children and their sleds rode a mechanical track down a glistening hill and around the back before appearing again at the top moments later. In the foreground, ice skaters skidded and twirled on a frozen pond. Benjamin, however, struggled to keep his focus off Elodie. How her face could still show such joy after the horrors she'd seen was a wonder. He could spend his whole life presenting her with simple pleasures if it meant seeing that gentle smile.

"I'd like to go sledding one day," she said. "It's been too long since I've gone."

"Next time it snows, I'll take you." The realization of what was to come struck him. Although Missouri was caught in a cold front, there was no more snow in the weather report. The likelihood of snow between now and the New Year was slim. It was high time he told her his news. Even if it might make her sad. Even if it would wreck her notion of having all her loved ones reunited in Hope Hill for the foreseeable future. He needed to tell her some time.

"I got a call—"

"I used to hate snow—"

They spoke at the same time, then chuckled together.

Elodie tucked her arm around his and pulled him along the sidewalk toward the next storefront. "I was saying I used to hate snow. After college, I thought joining the Army Nurse Corps for a stint in the Philippines would be heavenly. And for six weeks, it was. Sun, sand, and sea. I had these wild notions of adventure and romance."

Ben's chin jerked her way. Here, he'd been waiting for her to return to him after school, imagining a future for the two of them. No one was more shocked than he was to hear the announcement that she'd joined the military and accepted an assignment across the world. Yet she'd been so happy, he couldn't say a word. "When you shipped out, I was sure you'd meet someone. A doctor maybe. Or the rich owner of a sugar plantation. You'd have a tropical honeymoon then come back to Missouri a married woman."

Her cheeks lifted into a smile. "Me too. There was one man—a soldier from Fort Stotsenberg. He and I, along with another nurse and his friend, went picnicking on the beach one day. We had a grand time, splashing in the surf and relaxing beneath the palms. When the sun dipped low on the horizon, he kissed me."

The image slugged Ben hard in the belly so that the next breath seemed as far away as Bataan.

"Tuck was his name. From St. Louis. He was nice and polite, though a bit dull. Not very interesting to talk to. Whenever there was a lull in the conversation, he would point out all the different birds around us—their species and unique characteristics. He'd mimic their call even." Elodie's laugh was almost soothing enough to take away the ache. But then her smile fell. "As you might guess, it never went further than that one kiss. He asked me for a date, but I said no."

Her steps slowed in front of the next window. Inside, Santa Claus was placing presents beneath a Christmas tree. A model train circled the tree and passed by a toy gun. The lights on the tree glinted off the barrel of the rifle, draping it in red.

"The next time I saw him, he'd been hit with enough shrapnel to fill a gallon bucket—the result of one of the bombings on Corregidor. He didn't make it home to St. Louis." She blinked several times, forcing her tears to remain unshed.

"I'm sorry, Elodie." He placed his free hand over hers where it rested on his forearm. "Tuck seemed like a good guy."

"I didn't know him well, but he was nice enough. I only let him kiss me because—" Her lips closed, their heart shape reflecting in the glass.

Ben tucked her arm against his side. "You only let him kiss you because. . ."

She looked up at him and grinned. Either the red curtains surrounding the display cast a hue across her normally porcelain skin, or she was blushing. "Because he looked like you."

Chapter Four

With a flick of Elodie's wrist, the hammer came down on the nail's head lightly, just enough to break through the wood's surface. After a full day of serving medicine at the base hospital, it felt good to do something with her hands that required muscle and force.

"That should do it." Benjamin stepped onto the stage, gingerly at first. When the plywood didn't give way, he jumped a few times. He moved a few feet to the left and jumped again. The wood creaked. "I think we need another nail right here." From a tin, he grabbed a carpentry nail and placed its point in line with the others.

Elodie kneeled beside him, hammer in hand.

"Hit it," he said.

"What if I get your fingers?"

"I trust you." His innocent grin beamed as he pinched the nail to hold it steady.

A couple of taps set the nail. He slid his hand back, giving her room to dig the nail deep into the stud.

Before he could get away, she grabbed his hand and pressed it tight to the stage. She held the hammer up and gave a teasing smirk. "Hang on, one more hit." She pretended to zero the head of the hammer on his thumb.

He laughed as he recoiled, taking her hand with him. "Oh, I don't think so!"

As she had so many times in the past few weeks, she reflected on how their hands fit together. This time, however, he pulled away, folding his hands tightly on his lap.

"Benjamin Gabriel, what are you doing?"

"My hands are stained with grease."

"And?"

"I'm embarrassed."

"Embarrassed about holding down a good job that you love? And one you excel at? Nonsense."

"I just doubt a woman would want to hold one of these calloused paws in her dainty hand."

"Well, I wouldn't want you with a woman who whittled down all your expertise for building and fixing things into a little grease anyway."

"Yeah, you're pretty good at building things yourself." He stood and perused the stage around them. Satisfied, he rested his hands on his hips and nodded. "Looks good to me. What do you think?"

"It should work." Elodie pushed herself off the stage floor then dusted off her aching knees. The accomplishment she felt outweighed the sore muscles she had from five nights of stage-building. She also quite enjoyed the way Benjamin peered at her through the process of it. Impressed. Maybe proud. Not quite surprised, though. After all, they'd built a treehouse together when they were thirteen. Of all people, Benjamin knew her capabilities.

Time with Benjamin was soothing to her weary soul. All the world had expectations of her—her town, her family, even herself. Some expected her to act like a heroine straight out of the movie *So Proudly We Hail*. But Claudette Colbert she was not. Others treated her with such fragility—a victim of war. Still others, like Rhoda, resented her for circumstances Elodie had no control over.

Not Benjamin. Yes, he still looked out for her, pausing the work when her body weakened and bearing most of the heavy lifting, but he didn't coddle her or keep her wrapped in quilts. And to him, she was still plain old Elodie Wise. Anything heroic was attributed to the nursing profession in general.

He hopped off the stage then turned and held out his arms. "We're a great team."

"We are, aren't we?" She bent forward, placing her arms around his neck.

He gripped her waist and lowered her to the floor. Then, together they looked over their handiwork. The stage would be big enough for a band, and Clyde Irving would look excellent standing at the center.

She still couldn't believe her luck. Clyde Irving would be cohosting Hope Hill's fundraiser with her, all thanks to Benjamin. "Come on. I have a celebratory treat for us." She tugged him over to one of the round tables they'd borrowed from the Episcopal Church. They sat side by side in chairs dropped off by a group of high school teachers. Over the next two weeks, people all across town would deliver linens, decorations, dishes, and silverware, eager to help the returning soldiers in any possible way. From her purse, Elodie retrieved two bottles of Coca-Cola and a bottle opener. She popped the cap off one and offered it to him.

Benjamin's chuckle bounced off the high ceiling and the walls before settling deep within Elodie. "Don't mind if I do." He accepted the bottle but waited for her to remove her bottle cap. When she did, they clinked their soda pops together before taking a swig.

Elodie's eyes closed in surrender to the bubbly sweetness. Instantly, she was back on Leyte Island, just after liberation, tilting back the best Coca-Cola in the entire world. Even then, her thoughts had fallen on Benjamin. After all, it was his favorite drink, and they'd shared many.

She had wondered for the ten-thousandth time if he was still alive. She shook off the memory.

He slid a coin across the tabletop. "Penny for your thoughts."

"You never talk about your time in Europe."

His shoulders bobbed in a shrug. "Not much to tell. I had an assignment, and I did it. Nothing more, nothing less."

"An important assignment."

"Babysitting detail." His gave his head a small shake.

"A necessary duty." She studied his face as he stared down at the bottle in his hands. His dark lashes shielded his green eyes. How often had she imagined his face on every dying soldier she came across? She still felt the guilt-tinged relief when the man was *another* woman's dearest friend. "You told me that you, Clyde, and the production team stayed behind the lines, following the last of our troops after the battle ended. Were you ever in real danger?"

Benjamin scratched at his collar before lifting his eyes to her. Still, he was silent.

"You can tell me."

"Once. The crew wanted to get footage of Clyde flying a bomber, so we went up with a skeleton crew on a B-24." He seemed to chew his next words. "We were hit with some flak that killed one of the engines and tore up the fuel line. We had to land in enemy territory. Luckily, I was able to splice and reconnect the tubing. But some German soldiers came upon us. We exchanged gunfire, but in the end, we were able to get out of there."

"That's. . .that's amazing. Why didn't you ever tell me?"

"Clyde's studio made me sign a non-disclosure agreement. Some of that footage is supposedly in his movie."

"The one coming out soon? *Enemy Skies*?"

"That's the one."

Elodie swallowed hard. "Were you hurt?"

Benjamin tilted back the soda pop once more. If he thought she'd forget the question she asked, he had another think coming.

She nudged his foot with hers, although she wanted to stomp his toes for keeping this from her since she'd been back. "Tell me."

He heaved a deep breath. Then, after setting the bottle on the table, he squared his body to face her. He unfastened the top button of his grey coveralls, revealing his white undershirt. With the fingers of his left hand, he yanked the collar of his shirt out wide. The trapezius muscle above his clavicle was mangled, the skin surgically tied back together.

Elodie lurched forward, hoisting herself to her feet and into a nurse's posture. With the gentlest touch she could muster, she inspected the site. Thank the Lord, this bullet seemed to have gone cleanly through. Still, something clutched at her throat.

"It happened while I was working on the engine." He stretched his neck to the side so she could get the full view.

"When?"

"September 28 last year. That was Clyde's last mission. The studio decided that was enough, and he was discharged while I recovered."

"Does my family know?"

"No one does. Non-disclosure agreement, remember?"

"Why did you tell me?"

His shoulders rose and fell on his heavy breath. "Because I'm tired of keeping secrets from you."

"Oh, Benjamin." She could have lost him. Without thinking, her other hand cradled his neck. He turned to her. With only a few inches separating them, Elodie found something hidden in the depths of his eyes. Something she'd seen in glimpses before, but never like this. Never this strong. It called to her.

His hand reached toward her but paused midair. Waiting for permission, perhaps. To do what, though?

Noises from outside challenged the thudding of her heart.

Elodie straightened, turning her attention to the door of the hangar.

Muffled laughter sounded on the opposite side of the door, followed by a familiar booming voice.

"Swell. This is just swell," Benjamin said as he rebuttoned his coveralls.

When the door wrenched open, Clyde Irving strutted through.

Clyde Irving was confident, charming, and sociable on his best days, arrogant, smarmy, and brutish on his worst. He had the reputation of wooing every woman he worked with. And once he set his sights on something, he got it. Right now, he gaped at Elodie.

"Clyde, I wasn't expecting you so soon." Benjamin fought the temptation to step between Clyde and Elodie to break the trance the actor had fallen in.

"Well, old pal, I decided to clear off my schedule a bit and experience Christmas in the heartland. I hope you don't mind." Clyde sported a grin as big as the Hollywoodland sign itself.

"The heartland would love to have you spend the holidays here." Elodie's cheeks had pinked, and she sounded breathless.

Benjamin rubbed his neck where just minutes ago, Elodie had placed her hand. "Clyde Irving, this is Lieutenant Elodie Wise."

"Hello." Elodie offered a handshake.

True to his nature, Clyde took her hand, kissed it, and moved his chin in a slow circle, caressing her knuckles with his thin mustache. The same move Clyde used to bed women all over Europe. Ben couldn't feel queasier.

"Elodie, you are far more breathtaking than your picture."

Ben was wrong. A stronger wave of nausea roiled through him.

"My picture?"

Finally, Clyde shifted his gaze to Ben, letting a glimmer of mischief pass between them. "Well, your picture is all over. The youngest of the Battling Belles of Bataan? And the prettiest, if I do say so myself. Your reputation precedes you. You are quite the heroine, aren't you?"

"I didn't do anything that any other nurse wouldn't have done. In fact, of the nurses who were there with me, I probably did the least."

"El, don't sell yourself short." Ben wasn't sure Elodie heard him considering the way she studied Clyde's face.

"Thank you for coming out to help us raise money for the veterans," she said.

"Believe me, it's my honor. Besides, I missed my old friend here and wanted to come back and see him."

"It's good to see you too, Clyde. How are things going in California?"

"Sadly, not as much fun as usual."

"I find that hard to believe. You're always up for a good time."

"Maybe I'm maturing with age."

"Oh, I doubt that."

"Elodie, this is the site of the ball, correct?"

"Yes. Benjamin and I built this stage."

"You did a great job. You've got some muscles, don't you? Remind me not to get on your bad side."

"Elodie wouldn't hurt a fly."

"Pretty, strong, *and* sweet? I'm in love." A sly smile appeared on Clyde's face. When he spoke to her, his head dipped forward, breaking the gentlemanly plane between him and Elodie.

To Ben's dismay, Elodie wore that same sleepy smile as the women along the battle route in Europe. And Ben had also seen where those nighttime trysts led. He wouldn't let Clyde break Elodie's heart. And he certainly wouldn't let him use her the way he often did other women.

"Where are you staying?"

"We found a motor lodge a few miles from here."

"You should stay with me, Clyde," Benjamin said without thinking.

Elodie snickered. "Where's he going to sleep? You only have one room and one bed."

"I'll sleep on the floor. It's no problem." Ben had done it before, and he could do it again. Though this time, he feared something more dangerous than bombs falling on him.

"Clyde, my parents have an apartment over our garage. You are welcome to stay with us. They won't mind. It isn't the largest space, but it's better than a motor lodge."

"Sounds like we've figured it out, eh, Ben?" Clyde winked, and Ben felt his blood curdle.

Mr. and Mrs. Wise would love for that room to find use. They offered it to him when he returned from the front, but he hadn't wanted to inconvenience the family with his presence. Clyde didn't mind barging in at all.

"Gabriel. It's been a long time." The voice of Clyde's manager weaseled into Ben's ear from across the hangar.

Ben squeezed his eyes closed. Better and better. "Hello, Richard."

The man slithered in from the cold. He wore the same awful sports coat he'd worn during the campaign. Ben had never understood the motivation behind wearing that jacket while strutting past villagers who'd lost their homes, livelihood, and often, family members.

"We're glad you called." Richard pulled Ben's arm, forcing him to leave Clyde and Elodie to fawn all over each other. As if they wouldn't have plenty of time for that over the next two weeks. Once the couple was out of earshot, Richard spoke. "Clyde's gotten himself in some trouble in Hollywood recently. The long-legged variety. We need some good press. We drove past the theater on Main Street. I'm thinking we move the premiere of *Enemy Skies* to right here in Hope Hill."

"When?"

"December 22."

"The night before the fundraiser?"

"Yes. It'll bring in big stars and big money for Miss Wise's cause."

"Does *Lieutenant* Wise know?"

"I'm guessing Clyde's telling her as we speak."

Across the room, Elodie clapped a hand over her mouth. It would be a great thing to raise more money. The town would likely benefit from the press, and the businesses along Main Street would thrive. There wasn't a downside that Ben could see. Elodie caught his eye. When her hand lowered, he saw the biggest smile. No wonder Clyde was struck. She was pretty as an orchid in spring. And with this fundraiser coming together, she was in bloom.

"I know I can count on you to keep things straight here. I'll need your help with Clyde. I can't have him getting in trouble again. We need wholesome. We need goodness. We need purity." Richard's gaze fell on Elodie. "Yes, this should work out just fine. I'll set everything up with the theater. You keep an eye on Clyde as much as possible."

Still on babysitting detail. Now in his hometown. Ben clenched his fists and counted to twenty in his head. When that didn't dispel the anger, he lifted his eyes to the rafters.

Lord, help me get through this.

Richard glanced back at the small crew that had traveled with them—three men Benjamin didn't recognize. "Time to start making plans, boys." He joined them closer to the door.

Elodie bounced over to Ben, the happiest he'd seen her since she'd returned home. "Did you hear? About the premiere?" Her eyes glistened with unshed tears.

"I did. That'll be great. With all those funds coming in, you'll be able to help those soldiers."

"I know. And how exciting for the town as well!" Elodie sobered, lowering her voice. "Clyde asked if I'd accompany him to the premiere."

"As his date?"

"Yes, but not in a romantic way. It's Clyde Irving, after all."

"Exactly. It's Clyde Irving. Elodie. Be careful."

"Oh, please. I survived an internment camp. I think I can handle the wily ways of a Hollywood tomcat. I'm only going with him to bring more awareness to the needs of the soldiers."

"You're right. You can handle this. You already are. Everything is falling into place."

"You don't mind me stealing your girl for a night, do you, Benny-boy?" Clyde lifted one side of his iconic mustache. Because of him, countless actors had copied the same style.

Not Benjamin. He'd stay clean-shaven as a good soldier should.

"Elodie's her own person, and I support every decision she makes, especially if it will help a good cause."

"We'll make sure the charity is at the forefront because Lieutenant Elodie Wise said so. Gorgeous *and* sweet. No wonder Ben carried that picture of you during the war."

Ben's stomach dropped to his feet.

Elodie tilted her head. "Picture?" She pinned her focus on Ben.

"Ben carried a picture of you in his Bible over in Europe. If I asked him nicely, he would take it out and regale me with stories about the two of you."

Ben tried to swallow the putrid taste in his mouth. It did no good. As Clyde rambled on and on about what Hollywood royalty might attend the premiere and ball, Ben worked to keep his breaths steady. Elodie also remained quiet, until Clyde asked her for directions to her home. He'd grab his luggage from the lodge and be over soon. She offered step-by-step directions and politely escorted them out while Ben collected their tools and shut off the lights.

Outside the hangar, she stood peering up at the crystal-clear sky dotted with stars. It was late, with no trace of twilight left on the horizon. With no trace of the moon either, the darkness shrouded any emotion on her face. Ben placed his toolbox in the bed of his truck and joined her.

"El, I hope you aren't angry with me."

"Why would I be angry? Although I am curious. Was my picture the only one you had with you?"

"Yes."

She nodded. "The soldiers I tended often had pictures with them of someone back home. Sometimes they'd tell me all about her. Or stare at the picture during frightening times. I never imagined I'd be anyone's someone."

He longed to tell her everything he felt. But to her, they'd always just been friends.

"Did it help? To think of me?"

He recalled how the photograph felt warm between his fingers on the cold nights. How her eyes swept peace over him on the frightening days. How her smiling lips whispered promises of a possible future when the war seemed endless. "It did."

"Benjamin, is there anything you'd like to tell me?" She turned to him, her eyes as wide as he'd ever seen.

This was it. His moment to come clean. But telling her too much might jeopardize everything. She must feel it also. She looked pale even in this starlight, and her jaw was set at an awkward angle.

"There is something I need to tell you." He took a steadying breath. "I'm getting redeployed after the first of the year. To Japan."

Chapter Five

All at once, the Missouri ground seemed to crumble and sink to the earth's center, taking Elodie's heart with it.

"Japan?"

"Yeah. MacArthur put out a call a few months back for replacements for his Eighth Army to occupy Japan. With Fairfax Field halting operations for the Air Transport Command, I knew I'd be out of a job. So I reenlisted, and requested that assignment."

Elodie resisted the urge to take hold of his coat sleeves and cling to him. What would he make of that? "Why would you volunteer for that?"

Benjamin outstretched his hands, palms facing up. "I need to do something of value for our country."

"This all comes down to your inferiority complex? Freud and Adler would've had quite a time with you, Benjamin Gabriel." Elodie had seen the brutality of the war's Pacific Theater. The thought of Benjamin entering the land where those severe mentalities had originated did more than send shivers up her spine. It petrified her, and it took time for her voice to work once again. "How long have you known?"

"I found out the day before Thanksgiving."

"And you didn't tell me?"

"I was going to, but you said you were thankful for having everyone in your life together in one place. I didn't have the heart to ruin the holiday for you. And then there was all the excitement with the fundraiser. I figured I could help you pull this off, and maybe it would ease the jolt of my leaving."

"You think helping me raise money will make me feel better about the loss of the person I care most about in this world?" Elodie wiped away the tears.

She expected him to offer her a handkerchief or perhaps even brush the tears off her cheeks. Instead, Benjamin turned away, raking both of his hands through his dark hair.

"I guess you'll have to take that picture with you again."

"Not possible." When Benjamin faced her, the starlight passed over the twin canyons between his brows, leaving the darkness to fester. "It fell out of my Bible somewhere in France in the summer of '44."

Elodie made her best attempt at a smile. "I suppose I'll have to get you a new one to carry with you."

"I'd like that. But for now, we should get you back home. If your parents see Clyde Irving lurking around your house, they're likely to call the police. From what I gather, he doesn't need any more bad press."

"Nice house. Quaint." As he spoke, he wore a steady grin that Elodie couldn't read.

Her parents' house was surely a far cry from his California residence, but it was home.

"Thanks. Come on in, but be quiet. I need to tell my parents you'll be staying in the guest room, and they're likely asleep." Elodie led the way into the kitchen. "Stay here. I'll be right back."

At the top of the stairs, she rapped on her parents' door before opening it. It was dark in the room, but in the shadows, she saw two lumps. "Mama, Daddy?"

"What's wrong?" Mama asked, popping straight up in bed.

"Nothing, Mama. Clyde Irving came to town early. He's going to stay over the garage. Is that all right?"

"Clyde Irving, the movie star?" Her father roused more slowly.

"That's right."

"Where is he now?" Mama asked.

A scream broke through the dark, followed by a thump, a crash, then a manly groan.

"The kitchen," Elodie said as she darted out the bedroom door, then down the stairs.

Once she flipped on the light to the kitchen, she found Charlie, backed up against the sink with a book clutched to her chest. Clyde was on the floor, slumped against the refrigerator shelves with white liquid dripping off his signature hair and down over his mustache.

"What happened?" Elodie asked.

"He—he was rummaging through our refrigerator. I thought it was a burglar."

"Sweetheart, what burglar would steal a bottle of milk?" Daddy reached for a kitchen towel behind Charlie. He handed it to Clyde.

Clyde towel-dried his hair and face. "Actually, I was aiming for the ham. You didn't have to hit me with your book." He reached in the refrigerator, grabbed the paper-wrapped veal cutlets from the market, and pressed the package against the back of his head. "What is it? *War and Peace*?"

"*Gone with the Wind*."

"Figures. I give up the Rhett Butler role to Gable, and this is my payback."

Mama sighed loudly. "Charlie, say your apology."

"No. Why is he in our kitchen?"

"He's our guest." Elodie extended her hand to Clyde. "Mr. Irving, I'm sorry."

He accepted her hand and stood, wavering a bit until he steadied himself against the counter. "Call me Clyde."

"*Clyde* shouldn't be in our kitchen at eleven p.m." Charlie inspected her book for damage.

"*You* can call me Mr. Irving."

"I'll call you a taxi and send you right back to Hollywood," Charlie mumbled before strutting out of the kitchen.

"Your sister is. . .sweet," Clyde said to Elodie. "Is she single?"

Twenty minutes later, after Elodie had helped Clyde settle into his lodgings, she slid into bed next to Charlie.

"Is Hollywood all settled?" Charlie asked.

"He is. Sorry for frightening you."

"I'm tough."

Elodie mashed her lips together. Silence followed, and she urged the sob caught in her throat not to disturb it. She'd handled worse news than this before. But she'd never had her sister there to lean on. "Char—" The name cracked in half, and the first tears burst forth.

"What's wrong?" Charlie asked, pushing a lock of hair off Elodie's cheek.

"Benjamin told me he's getting transferred."

"Oh, I see."

"Did you know?"

"I did. I'm glad he finally told you."

"Charlie, I'm so sad."

"Of course you are. You love him."

Elodie nearly laughed. "That's true. He's the brother I always wanted."

"No, he's the brother *I* always wanted. For you, it's different."

"What do you mean?" The chill in the room raised gooseflesh on Elodie's arms beneath her nightgown. She pulled Charlie's blanket up to her chin.

"I see the way you two look at each other. Like a walk down the aisle is the next logical step."

"You're silly. Not Benjamin and I."

"Have you ever imagined kissing him?"

"Charlie!" Elodie squealed into her sister's pillow. "You shouldn't say such things!"

"Have you?"

She'd imagined it just tonight when she'd seen where a bullet had tried to take his life. Elodie rolled onto her back and stared at the dark ceiling. "Maybe. He carried a picture of me during the war. Clyde told me. The men in my ward carried pictures of their sweethearts all the time. I knew what it meant to them. I never imagined Benjamin saw me like that until tonight."

"He loves you, El. It's clear to everyone but you. What you two have is already pretty special. Imagine what it could be."

"That's what I'm afraid of. What if I begin to see him in that way, and then he leaves in three weeks?" Tears burned Elodie's eyes once again. "What good is imagining what can never be?"

Chapter Six

Ben's focus burned straight through the windshield to the road ahead. Anything to keep from seeing in the rearview mirror the way Clyde poured his attention on Elodie, inching closer to her with every turn. It was enough to drive a man mad.

"So I said, 'I don't care if you are Frank Capra. I'm not dancing a jig with a poodle!' Everyone on set busted a gut," Clyde said.

"I bet they did." Elodie's voice, as always, held a polite lilt. She had to be as bored by Clyde's endless rambling as Ben was.

A laugh burst from the passenger seat—an exaggerated guffaw that rattled the seats more than the potholes did. "Tell us more about all the famous people you know, Hollywood. Maybe a bit more about Katherine Hepburn's dog. Or Gregory Peck's bathtub. It's all incredibly fascinating."

"Charlotte Jessalyn Wise," Elodie scolded.

"Yes, Mother?"

Ben pulled the car into a parking space. "We're here." And not a moment too soon. If Clyde wanted a night out on the town, he'd get it. And luckily, it wouldn't take long for him to experience all the nightlife Hope Hill offered. But then again, Ben wasn't in a rush to drop Elodie and Clyde off at her house to continue his flirtations late into the night. Maybe he should've driven them all the way into Kansas City. Topeka, even.

"The Barking Beagle?" Clyde asked.

Charlie twisted in her seat to face Clyde. "It may not have swanky enough clientele for the likes of you, Hollywood, but it has good food and even better music."

"You don't think much of me, do you, Charlie?"

"Oh, Clyde. You think about yourself enough for both of us."

Ben bit his bottom lip to keep his snicker at bay. He opened his car door and stepped out into the crisp Missouri air. Not as cold as a week ago when he and Elodie had been on this same street buying her family's Christmas tree and taking in the window displays, but still frosty enough to nip at his nose.

He held the door for Elodie. Fortunately, Clyde had removed his mitts from her shoulder long enough for her to step out of the car.

"Thanks for driving, Benjamin."

"Happy to."

"And thanks for coming along. I don't want Clyde thinking this is a date."

Benjamin leaned in close. "Considering how he kept pawing at you, I don't think he got that telegram."

Inside The Barking Beagle, the light struggled to cut through the smoky haze. Still, it was bright enough for Ben to note how many liquor-filled glasses covered the tables. Clyde seemed to notice too, considering how he worked his lips. Ben had his work cut out for him tonight.

The foursome nabbed a table on the edge of the dancefloor where a few couples swayed to "It's Been a Long, Long Time." Elodie watched them for several moments before dragging her gaze down across the table then up to Ben's eyes. When he caught her glance, she turned away, touching her cheeks with her fingertips. Their pale polish contrasted sharply to the rouged color rising to her face.

They hadn't spoken about the photograph since Thursday night. The topic hung heavily between the two of them. At least it hadn't frightened her away. They'd worked all day in the hangar painting the stage, and she hadn't once looked at him like he was a creep. In fact, the day had comprised of small glimpses, almost curious in nature. Like he was a puzzle piece she was trying to place.

"Looking to wet your whistle?" The waitress's final word faded as she recognized Clyde's mug.

"Certainly." Clyde sang the title line to the Andrews Sisters' "Rum and Coca-Cola."

"Give us a minute, will ya?" Benjamin waited for the waitress to stumble away before addressing Clyde. "How about we stay dry tonight, eh, Clyde?"

"Where's the fun in that?" Clyde winked at Elodie.

"Christmas in the heartland. Isn't that what you said you wanted? I think it's best we leave the alcohol for the other patrons."

Clyde rolled his eyes but settled for a Coca-Cola without the rum. He was drunk enough on the attention of the others in the place. At least half a dozen times someone asked him for an autograph or handshake. Clyde was keen to oblige.

Not everyone appreciated the fanfare, though. Charlie had been bumped and bustled in each one of the encounters—something that appeared to amuse Clyde quite a bit.

"Do we have a backup plan for a celebrity host?" Elodie's whispering breath tickled Ben's neck marvelously. "Charlie might just kill Clyde before we get to the twenty-third."

"Well, if she does, she'll have to dress up as him."

"A little hair dye and a cut? That's doable. The mustache will be tougher." She bumped his shoulder with hers. The smile she offered may as well have seeped into his very soul. For the first time since Thursday, she held his gaze, until a hand reached in front of her.

"Let's dance." Clyde stood above Elodie—more than six feet of leading man interrupting their moment.

The band played the first few notes of Glenn Miller's "In the Mood."

"I'm not a great dancer," she said.

"I am." Clyde grabbed her hand and tugged her from the seat. On the dance floor, he took her in his arms and began rocking her back and forth, then swinging her to and fro.

The hollowing ache in Benjamin's chest conflicted with the happiness at seeing the joy on Elodie's face. Pure delight. Around them, the crowd cheered. Clyde's smooth steps and eager expression only urged them on. A light flashed—a photographer's bulb from the far side of the bar.

Ben could only swig his soda pop. Meanwhile, Charlie was all smiles.

"What are you so happy about?" he asked.

"Have you any idea how much publicity this will bring to the ball? That's the reason why Clyde's here, isn't it? This is fantastic."

"For the soldiers, sure."

"And for us. Elodie needs this. She needs to see that our citizens will look after the soldiers if she doesn't. Only then will she be able to move on with her own dreams."

"Is one of her dreams to take up with a movie star?"

"Of course not. But would it be so bad if this opened her eyes to the love story she's meant to have?"

Ben scoffed. "You forget. I know Clyde. He always wins. He gets the glamour, the glory, and the girl. Every time."

Charlie patted his shoulder. "Not this time. Have a little faith."

The next morning, Ben awoke to see the local newspaper jutting beneath the door to his room. He rubbed the sleep from his eyes, threw off his covers, and sat up in bed. The first rays of sunlight sprayed through his window and honed in on the picture taking up space beneath the headline. Elodie smiled as her pin curls froze midmotion. In the arms of someone whose face was blocked by the door. Ben fell back onto his bed, covered his head with his pillow, and groaned.

Chapter Seven

E lodie stared into the dress shop's fitting room mirror, tugging at the loose folds of fabric. There was a time she might have filled out this dress. But her three-year-long death march of starvation and disease had robbed her of her once-ample curves. At least she'd survived. Others hadn't been so fortunate.

Tremors in her fingers released the silky material. Would they ever stop? Might she ever look back at her time in the war and not quake with panic? Elodie stretched her hand taut and silently sang:

The Lord is my light
and my salvation;
who-oom shall I fear?
the Lord is the strength of my life...

The verse was enough to ease the trembling. Once again, she took in her reflection. If there were a way to bring more focus on the Heroes ball without her name in lights, she'd surely do it. Perhaps she could keep her coat on the whole time. It would be cold on the red carpet as well as in the drafty old movie house. She'd just seen a picture of Rita Hayworth at her premiere. Because of the fur coat, you couldn't see her dress at all.

No doubt, all eyes would be on her. Especially after this morning's newspaper article. And that headline? *Clyde Irving Woos Bataan Belle*? Absurd. That morning at church, she'd had no luck getting the editor to consider a retraction. News was news, whether it was steeped in facts or not. And as Charlie told her as they fell asleep, this kind of publicity could only benefit Elodie's cause.

"El, are you decent?" Charlie called from behind the curtain.

"You could say that."

"Good. Ben's here. He says something bad has happened."

"What?"

"He wouldn't tell me, but he said it's about the dance."

Elodie pushed back the curtain and hurried out of the dressing room, still wearing the premiere dress. Sure enough, Ben stood near one of the dress forms, his face wrenched into a grimace. But when he saw her, his sorrowful expression faded away at once. As she neared, his lips shaped themselves to make words, but alas, no sound came.

She folded her hands again and again. "What's happened?"

He stepped nearer. "Elodie, you look. . .beautiful."

Holding her arms outstretched, she took a gander at herself. She felt naked with no hose or shoes on. But there was something about his compliment when she wasn't completely covered and done up that warmed her from the inside out. And the way he looked at her just now? It made her wonder if Charlie was right about his feelings.

She gathered a breath and lifted a curl off her face. "Thank you, Benjamin."

He nodded but stood in place.

"What's happened?" she repeated.

The question broke whatever trance he'd fallen into, and the frown returned. "There's a storm over the Pacific. The soldiers—the local guys we're honoring at the ball—are on a ship that's been detoured through calmer waters. They'll be landing on American soil a couple of days late. And rumor has it that soldiers are struggling to get out of port cities. Everyone's trying to get home for Christmas, and it's caused major traffic jams at airports and train stations. And with Christmas only nine days away, it's only going to get worse."

Elodie clenched her arms across her stomach, but they yielded no comfort. "That's why we're doing all this. If they aren't here, it will be for nothing." She squeezed her eyes closed.

A warm palm rested on the side of her neck. When her eyes opened, Ben was close enough for Elodie to see the tiny scar on his chin from when he'd fallen out of their treehouse years ago. What strange comfort this familiarity was when everything between them seemed to be changing.

"It won't be for nothing, I assure you." He leaned in, cutting the space in half. "You've inspired all of us to get involved. And the money will be waiting for them when they get here, whether that's for Christmas or not."

The night's soft breeze sifted through her layers, and Elodie pulled her coat closed over her ward dress. Still, the walk home from her shift felt good, even as the day gave way to night. A streetlamp caught the last remaining leaves on the tree branches—the stubborn ones trying with all their might to survive until spring. Not unlike her own prayer in Santo Tomas. *Help me survive this day, Lord.* She hadn't the faith to trust Him for three years, but one day? That much faith she had.

From a medical standpoint, the past two days at the hospital had been uneventful. Dull, even. She liked dull. She'd learned her lesson from wanting more out of life. After all, that was what had brought her to the Philippines in the first place—the dream of an exciting adventure. She now understood the beauty of the mundane, although she did wish to do more for her patients than merely hand them a cup with medication in it.

But from a gossip standpoint, the past two days had been anything but uneventful. Whispers and side glances between her fellow nurses were enough to boil her blood. Truth be told, she had no interest in Clyde Irving. Perhaps she'd once been curious about him. What young female wouldn't be? But she'd seen enough these past five days to satisfy that niggling. Clyde was egocentric and a showboat. There was absolutely zilch that was genuine or authentic. And apart from an appreciation to him for coming here, she felt nothing toward the man.

Elodie neared the entrance to her family's driveway. The warm glow reached through the windows into the night, drawing her home. Oh, how she'd missed this place and the people in it. She checked her watch, tilting it, so the face caught the light from the front porch—a quarter past six. Dinner would be ready soon.

Inside the family room window, she saw Clyde's profile. Her family had welcomed him in, personality flaws and all. They were kind like that.

Elodie heaved a deep breath. She didn't want to entertain Clyde tonight. There was someone else she wanted to spend the evening with instead. Someone whose residence she'd passed by four blocks back. Someone with a knack for always saying the right thing at the right time.

She reached for the front door handle, but before she could touch it, the door swung open.

Benjamin stood, blocking the frame. "There you are. Your mother was worried, so I was coming to look for you."

"I walked instead of taking the bus."

He stepped out of her way, then shut the door after her. He helped her with her purse and coat, hanging them on the rack. When Elodie shivered, his warm hands slid up her arms and down again. "Cold walk?"

"Yes, it was. But this helps." Had he always had such nice lips? Gracious. Now she was staring at his lips. She forced down a swallow. "What are you doing here?"

"I'm supposed to keep an eye on Clyde, remember?"

"What kind of trouble will he get into here?"

"With Rhoda and Charlie? Who knows?" He pressed his lips together for a brief moment. "Guess I also wanted to see you. I've only got a little more time to spend with you, so. . ."

"I'm glad you did."

"Elodie Lila Wise, is that you?" her mother asked from the direction of the kitchen.

"Yes, Mama. I'm sorry I didn't phone."

"Don't apologize to me. Apologize to my poor nerves."

Over a meal of meatloaf, mashed potatoes, and creamed spinach, Elodie's family listened to Clyde's tales about high jinks on movie sets. Equally entertaining were the various expressions Charlie employed while listening to them. Ben also enjoyed the show, tapping Elodie's knee beneath the table whenever an especially eccentric look appeared on her sister's face.

"What can you tell us about *Enemy Skies*? We're all looking forward to the premiere. Were there any funny stories filming?" Rhoda asked.

Clyde wiped his mouth with a napkin. "Most of the movie was filmed on a soundstage in Los Angeles, but as Ben here can attest, there were several scenes filmed in actual combat."

Ben shifted in his seat, keeping his head low.

"Filming that, as you can imagine, was a bit more somber," Clyde explained.

"That was very brave of you, Clyde, joining the war effort. I'm glad neither you nor Ben were hurt," her mother said.

Elodie stiffened.

"That isn't exactly true," Clyde said. "Combat was harder than I expected. You fought, didn't you, Mr. Wise?" Clyde sneezed, setting loose a dark lock of hair into his eyes. "I apologize. I—" Again, he sneezed.

"I hope you aren't getting sick ahead of your movie premiere," her father said.

"I'll be fine, Mr. Wise. Thank you for your concern."

Rhoda, sitting at Clyde's side, stared down at her plate with disgust. "Ew. Clyde sneezed on my dinner. Can I be done?"

Once the dishes had been collected, Benjamin began washing them. Elodie joined him, drying the plates and silverware with a dishtowel. She'd suddenly become more aware of him, the way he moved about the kitchen. And how masculine his hands looked covered with soap bubbles. She found herself mesmerized by the way the muscles in his forearms worked as he scrubbed her mother's plates.

"Elodie, are you listening?"

How many times had her mother called her name? "Yes, Mama?" Elodie turned, knowing full well her face was burning as red as the dishtowel in her hand.

"Bob Hope's on the radio. He's recording from San Francisco. Rhoda's turning it on now. When you and Ben are finished, you should join us in the family room."

She nodded, then rested her hand on his bicep. "Do you need to head home yet?"

"I'm in no hurry."

"Good." Elodie took the last dish from him, drying it as he drained the sink. She opened the cabinet. The spot for the dish was too high for her reach.

"I'll get that." Benjamin took the dish, his fingers dragging against hers in the process. He stretched, bringing his body closer to hers, and stealing her breath in the process. After he'd placed the dish and closed the cabinet, he grabbed her hand. "Ready for some laughs?"

From her spot next to Ben on the couch, Elodie laughed so hard she had tears spouting from the corner of her eyes as Bob Hope and company acted out a scene. Even Rhoda chuckled a few times, although she didn't seem to like how close Elodie was to Ben. Not that they had a choice. With Clyde sitting on her right and Charlie at the far end, the sofa was cramped.

Skinnay Ennis sang a new song, "Let It Snow, Let It Snow, Let It Snow," while Mrs. Wise handed glasses of eggnog to each person.

"This song is terrible. It will never catch on," Clyde said before unleashing yet another sneeze. His eggnog sloshed over the side of his glass, splattering on his trousers.

Elodie placed the back of her hand on Clyde's forehead. "You have a fever, Clyde. Do you have chills or aches at all?"

"A bit." Clyde handed the drink back to Mrs. Wise. "I think I'll turn in a bit early." Clyde stood. With a cordial bow, he excused himself through the back door.

When Elodie didn't move from her seat next to Ben, a new joy that had nothing to do with Bob Hope's humor flooded through him.

After the radio show ended, Mrs. Wise yawned. "Time we head to bed. Rhoda, you too."

"Mama, I'm eighteen. I can stay up."

"Young lady..." Mr. Wise's final syllable rose in both pitch and warning, prompting the youngest daughter to stomp out of the room. "Charlie, please check on Mr. Irving. See if he needs anything."

"Why? He's a grown man."

"He's our guest," Mrs. Wise said.

"Why me? Elodie's the nurse in the family."

Mr. Wise lowered his stare on Charlie, who promptly rolled her eyes. "Right away. I'll be sure to fluff his pillow. . .right over the top of his smug face."

"Oh, Charlotte." Mrs. Wise shook her head.

Charlie stuffed her arms into her sweater and went to the back door. With the door handle in her hand, she turned. "I'd take his temperature, but we already know he's full of hot air." She was out the door before her parents could respond.

Meanwhile, Elodie buried her face into Ben's shoulder, which did nothing to hide the laughter shaking her torso.

"These daughters of ours. Nat, I blame you," Mrs. Wise said to her husband. "At least we have Benjamin to keep things on the up and up. Don't stay up too late, you two."

"We won't. Goodnight," Ben said.

"Are they gone?" Elodie asked, peeking from Ben's shoulder.

"Yeah. It's just us."

"Good." She lifted her chin, then rested it on his shoulder. "Sometimes I like it better this way."

"Me too."

Over the radio, the lyrics of "I'll Be Home for Christmas" plucked at Ben's heart.

Elodie adjusted her head until her cheek rested against him. "We were allowed to listen to some American radio occasionally at the camp. Our captors couldn't give us enough food to nourish us, but they'd allow us to listen to music." Half a laugh followed her words past her lips. "When this song played, the whole camp went silent."

"It always made me think of you. Sure, I wanted to come home. But more than that, I wanted to be wherever you were." He chewed his lip, urged his breathing to remain steady. His hand sat awkwardly on his thigh, mere inches from hers. Close, but not together.

She sat up, inviting space between the two of them. Worry wrought her brow. "I'm ashamed to say I wanted you there with me too. Isn't that awfully selfish? That at one point, I wished you were one of the soldiers under my care, even knowing that would have meant starvation and disease? But at least then, I could've had you in my keeping. I could've had a confidante. Someone who understood. So selfish."

"That doesn't make you selfish, El. It makes you human."

Her gaze fell to her trembling hands in her lap. She extended her fingers, keeping them taut. "My parents don't understand. Every night, my mother checks on me as I sleep. She opens the door, then leaves the hall light on—a nightlight of sorts, thinking it will help. I know she means well, but it's strange. I'm more frightened in the light than the total darkness."

"Because of the blackouts." Ben sighed. He held out his hand, and she matched her fingers to his. "Light made you a target during the bombings on Bataan and Corregidor, didn't it? It was the same for us in Europe. Even the smallest light felt like a threat."

"Yes." Her soft voice weaved through his thoughts. Whatever she wanted, whatever she needed at this moment, he'd offer. If only he could read her mind.

The back door slammed. Charlie groaned. "That boorish, insolent, no-good, grandstanding crumb of a man." She never even looked their direction as she clomped through the room and up the stairs in the foyer.

Elodie's focus drifted back to Ben. She waited on something, though he wasn't sure what.

Sucking in a deep breath, he angled his body toward her, lifted his arm, and placed it on the back of the couch. "Come here."

She didn't hesitate to settle against his chest. He tucked her close to him. It took a few songs and a couple of commercials for their breaths to sync in a slow, steady rhythm. When she began to snore ever so slightly, he felt his heart surrender to her completely.

How was he supposed to leave for Japan now?

Chapter Eight

Elodie knocked on the door to the guest room, the handles of the soup bowl nearing the point of scalding by the time Clyde opened the door. When he did, she burst past him and set the bowl on the bedside table.

Clyde cleared his throat. "Well, come on in, why don't you?"

She turned back to face him. He wore a white undershirt, untucked over a pair of trousers. His bare toes stuck out from beneath the hems. The man should be wearing socks on a day like today. "I brought you chicken soup. Mama wholeheartedly believes that will fix you right up. How are you feeling?"

"I think I'm through the worst of it. It no longer feels like an army is marching through my head." He grinned. Even sick, he hadn't lost his charm. Or his looks. With his hair falling over his forehead instead of slicked back with pomade, he looked like a younger, more innocent version of the Hollywood leading man he was recognized to be.

She pushed his hair back and felt above his brow. Nice and cool, though a bit clammy. "Feels like the fever broke. I believe you should be just fine to attend the premiere tomorrow night. The whole town is buzzing over the celebrities arriving. They've never seen such fancy cars."

"Glad to hear it. How are final preparations for the dance coming? Just about forty-eight hours to go, right? Or has my foggy brain got my days mixed up?"

"Close enough. Tomorrow, my family and several others in the community are meeting at the hangar to put everything in place." Out of habit, Elodie straightened the bedsheets.

"Maybe I'll come by if I'm on the mend. Any news on the transport of soldiers?"

Elodie paused. Was Clyde Irving concerned about someone other than himself? The question both warmed and confused her. "They're still at a repatriation center in San Francisco. They were able to get seats on a bus, though, and should arrive at the hangar during the ball. That's nice of you to ask about them."

Clyde scrubbed his hand across his unshaven jaw. "I hope you'll still be my date for the premiere."

"Date? Clyde, what the papers are saying about us being a couple. . . I don't want to fuel those rumors. But I'll attend the premiere as your guest."

Clyde cocked his head. "Is this because of Benny?"

Warmth gripped Elodie. "Perhaps. He's my dearest friend. And he's leaving soon." Her throat tightened with the admission. "I'd like to have him at my side as well, if you don't mind. I'll walk the red carpet with you, but I'd like to sit with him during the movie."

"I don't mind at all. I understand. I'm not sure I could've done what I did over there if I hadn't had him around like I did. He inspired courage in me that I'd never had before."

"Oh yeah?"

"Sometimes at night, it got too quiet. Whenever I got to talking about the point of it all, he never told me to shut my trap. Instead, he encouraged me to keep gnawing on it. The truth is, sometimes the fame and glory don't feel like enough. Anyway, I've said too much."

Elodie rested her hand on his arm. "After you eat, if you're feeling up to it, we're going caroling in town."

"I'm still gathering my strength. And I'm not much for caroling."

"Okay. Charlie will stop by later to check on you then."

Clyde's smooth grin fell in one swoop.

Ben shouldn't be expected to get anything done when Elodie was nearby. Even a task as simple as decorating the donated Christmas tree on the hangar's stage was more difficult when all his concentration was on her small movements.

"Whoever invented tinsel is surely laughing now at the mess they've created." He pulled a silver thread from its bundle and laid it across a branch.

"All right. Who replaced my Benjamin with Ebenezer Scrooge?" Elodie took a piece of tinsel and draped it over Ben's ear.

"Don't start, Wise."

She pursed her lips and held up another piece above his head. It caught in his hair, and an end fell between his eyes.

"That's it." He dropped the handful of tinsel. When she squealed and ran down the steps of the stage, he followed her, nearly clipping Mr. Wise as he nailed the curtain to the front of the stage Ben and Elodie had built. "Sorry, Mr. Wise!"

Elodie hid behind Charlie, who was carrying a large stack of folded tablecloths.

"Don't use me as a shield," Charlie said, hurrying out of the way and leaving her sister exposed.

Benjamin pounced, but Elodie ducked out of his reach. He followed her to the vacant floor space near the back, where he grabbed her around the waist and spun her in a circle. Her laugh bounced off the steel walls. When he set her feet back on the ground, she turned into him, giggling against his neck most fantastically.

On Ben's right, something clattered on the concrete. There, Rhoda stood above a dropped push broom, glaring at Elodie.

"It's not enough to steal all the attention. You have to steal Ben too?" Rhoda ran to the exit door while the rest of the volunteers watched the scene.

Elodie moved to follow her, but Ben caught her wrist.

"Let me talk to her first," he said.

Compassion swirled in her eyes. "Okay. Be gentle with her. Not that you'd ever need that reminder." A tiny slice of tinsel had threaded itself into the curl in front of her ear.

Benjamin carefully removed it before grinning and excusing himself. He grabbed his coat from the stack by the door and stepped into the deceptive December sun. It may look warm, but that ice-blue sky wasn't playing games. He glanced around. "Where'd you go, Rhoda?"

From the far side of the lot, a metal barrel drummed and rocked a bit. Behind it, a bobby-socked and saddle-shoed foot slid out of view. Ben jogged toward it.

Rhoda had her hands crossed over her stomach. Already, she was shivering. Twin trails of tears streaked her face.

Ben spread his coat wide and placed it over her.

"Thank you."

"You got it." He took a seat on the gravel and allowed the chittering of a field critter to fill the silence for thirty seconds while he thought of what to say. "I bet it hasn't been easy for you."

Rhoda stared straight ahead, her chin trembling slightly. She sniffed, then pulled her legs up to her chest, using the coat as a blanket.

"I remember how close you and Elodie were before she left for Manila. It was hard having her leave, wasn't it? I know I felt like that. Getting left behind never feels good."

When her face crumpled, Ben put his arm around her shoulder. Rhoda sniffled. "I was so mad. I wanted something bad to happen to her. Then when it did. . ."

"You blamed yourself? Rhoda, that's not why she was taken prisoner."

"Then why was she?"

Ben fumbled for a word, any word at all. But how many times had he asked God the same question?

Rhoda heaved a breath. "Once she was taken to that camp, Elodie was all anyone cared about. We didn't celebrate anything. Not birthdays or holidays. Only anniversaries for Elodie's enlistment, deployment, and capture. Those, Mama treated like funerals. And everything was about sacrifice for the war effort. Everyone said it was my duty, but I never signed up for that." Rhoda wiped her nose on his coat—a move that might have made him laugh in other circumstances. "And then she came home, but still it was all about her. Finally, we get a Christmas without war, but here we are, giving more of our time to Elodie and her dreams. Why don't I get to have the goals and the dreams and the romance?"

"You do get to have that, Rhoda. After tomorrow, it will be different. You'll see. And George Weston will be coming home, right?"

"What does that have to do with anything?"

"I've seen those letters from him sitting on the table. And the outgoing ones with the heart over the *i* in Wise." He squeezed her tight.

"Ben!" Her face flamed bright pink.

"I'm just saying you have a lot of great things coming your way. And you may not see it now, but you're fortunate to have your sisters."

"Even Charlie?"

"Even Charlie. Come on. Let's head back in and get warm."

As they walked back toward the hangar, Rhoda kept tight to Ben's side. "Hey, Ben, if Elodie chooses Clyde, do I get you?"

He chuckled. "Oh, Rhoda. . ." He held the door open for her, then stepped inside, perusing the scene until he spied Elodie.

She was up on a ladder finishing the tree trimming. Clyde stood off to the side with his hand on the small of her back. When Elodie saw him, she turned a bit, and Clyde's hand moved to her hip.

Ben worked to loosen his clenched fists as he approached the two of them.

"Is Rhoda okay?" Elodie asked.

"She will be. The place looks almost ready. Everyone is packing up, I see."

"This is the final touch." Elodie held up a star tree topper. "Star or Angel?"

Clyde removed his hand from Elodie and held up a knit angel.

"Angel. Always," Ben said.

"I had a feeling you'd say that," Clyde said. He lifted the topper to Elodie.

She placed the angel on top of the tree. "Perfect. We're all ready for tomorrow."

Clyde lifted Elodie down from the ladder. "Excellent. It's nearly time for your red carpet debut, Lieutenant Wise."

Chapter Nine

O ver the span of a few hours, her small town had been transformed into Tinseltown. The movie house had been scrubbed and painted. The burned-out bulbs surrounding the marquee had been replaced, and Clyde Irving's name, along with the film's title, *Enemy Skies,* shone brightly above the red carpet.

Inside the car, Elodie adjusted her gloves where they bunched on her wrists.

"You look ravishing, my dear," Clyde said.

"I'm not sure why I must walk the red carpet. Are you sure this will help bring attention to the needs of our soldiers?"

"Trust me. It'll do wonders for the charity." He took her hand. "Let's go shine."

As Elodie followed Clyde out of the car, flashbulbs, reporters, and a film camera bombarded them. A blond woman she recognized as a famous actress—what was her name again?—pushed her way in between Elodie and Clyde.

"Hi, doll. Patricia Ridgeway, I'm sure you know. Listen, hon, I'm interested in playing you in an upcoming film."

"Patricia, please. This isn't the time," Clyde warned. He tugged Elodie past the woman.

There was too much noise. Too many flashes. People crowded her, and she lost Clyde's hand. The scene spun, and she was back on

Corregidor, dodging debris and explosions. It was challenging to find breath amidst the chaos. If only there were someone she could help. Then, maybe she'd find her way through.

Past the faces, some familiar, others not, she caught sight of Benjamin. All it took was one glance, and soon he was right at her side, shielding her from the bulk of the intruders. Still, breath eluded her.

"Lieutenant Wise?" Through the commotion, a motherly voice broke through. It belonged to a short woman who might have once had a friendly face before war riddled the world. Her brow hung heavy over weathered eyes that wore sorrow like a cloak.

Elodie was drawn to her. "I'm Lieutenant Wise."

"I'm sorry to bother you, especially on a night like this. My name is Florence Uchermann. My son served in Manila before the war began. Sadly, we received word that he was killed early in '42."

A hand to her chest did nothing to soothe the pain Elodie felt pierce her heart over the woman's loss. So many had died, yet the loss of even one life still shattered. "I'm so sorry."

"We know nothing else. I was hoping you might have run into him. His name was Tom."

Benjamin whispered in Elodie's ear. "You don't have to help her."

"It's okay." Elodie searched her trembling hands like they might hold an answer for this woman. She'd seen thousands upon thousands of soldiers during her tour of duty. Tom. Tom Uchermann. Her breath rushed out, carrying one name with it. "Tuck."

"Yes, Tuck was his nickname at Fort Stotsenberg. Did you know him?"

"A little. He and I picnicked together on Thanksgiving Day of '41." Elodie felt a smile stretch her lips even as tears filled her eyes. "I liked him."

Tuck's mother smiled as well. "He was a good boy. Everyone liked him. Can you tell me anything else?"

Benjamin took Elodie's hand, steadying it as she pondered what she might say to a mourning mother.

"I didn't see him again until he was brought into the ward we'd set up in the jungle that January. He'd been gravely injured, but he wasn't in pain. He'd received morphine, but he was still lucid. I held his hand, and he spoke of fishing the Mississippi with his father and your dancing lessons beneath a weeping willow."

His mother's chin quivered. Elodie released Benjamin's hand and took both of Florence's in hers. "I'll never forget his last words. He smiled up at the palm fronds above him and said, 'I sure would like to dance again.' And he was gone."

Mrs. Uchermann closed her eyes, and tears fell, creating tiny starbursts on the red carpet down below their interlocked hands. The noise surrounding them had hushed at some point. Every person stilled, listening to their conversation. Every person except Benjamin, who tugged a handkerchief from his pocket and held it out to the woman. She accepted it, but when she noticed Benjamin, perhaps for the first time, she froze.

"You look very much like my Tom." She studied his face, placing a hand on his cheek and turning his head. Benjamin obliged, and when new tears came, he covered her hand with his.

Elodie sniffled. "This is Benjamin Gabriel, my closest friend. He fought alongside Clyde Irving in France."

Mrs. Uchermann nodded. She dabbed the handkerchief against each eye, then offered it back to Ben.

"Keep it, in case the tears keep coming," he said.

"Thank you. Both of you. You've brought much peace to an old mother's heart."

"Will you stay for the movie?" Elodie asked.

"No, I've had enough war. I think I'll return home and finally lay Tom down to rest."

Elodie and Benjamin watched her slip through the crowd. Once she'd disappeared, Elodie's lungs opened, and she could breathe again. She shared a glance with Benjamin, but it was short-lived as Clyde stepped between them.

Clyde took Elodie's hand. "Time to head inside. My movie's about to start."

Enemy Skies was precisely the kind of film audiences needed one year ago. A final push to support the troops to finish the race and bring home the victory. But now, the battle scenes and trauma felt gratuitous. Then again, Ben wasn't a filmmaker.

Clyde played a soldier named Edmond, who falls for Marguerite, a French nurse who is betrothed to a Nazi officer. The crowd oohed and aahed at all the right moments, even if it was fantastically unrealistic.

Elodie sat between Ben and Clyde in the front row. She seemed unimpressed by Clyde's performance. Whenever the battle scene did bend toward reality, she leaned Ben's way, not Clyde's.

Most of the scenes were filmed on a stage, but a good deal of footage from their time in Europe had been added. Every familiar scene gave Ben a jolt. He could still smell the concrete dust, feel the smoldering heat from the dashed fires, and see the tear-streaked faces of the people offscreen.

One particular scene gutted Ben. Edmond laments the horrors of war in the rubble of a French church. In actuality, it had been Ben who'd let loose his prayers of abandon in that church. Some of the lines Clyde's character spoke were too close to Ben's heart, stolen from his most vulnerable moments. He'd only pulled himself back together when something in the rubble reminded him of Elodie.

He shifted in his seat.

"Are you doing all right?" Elodie whispered.

One look at her soft eyes and one whiff of her flowery perfume steadied him. She turned her hand palm up on the armrest, stretching her delicate fingers to their full length. He slid his hand over hers, fingertip to fingertip.

"I am now," he said, interlocking their fingers.

As the film headed toward its climax, anti-aircraft flak hit the engine of the bomber Edmond flew in. Sure enough, the plane went down behind enemy lines. While the rest of the soldiers provided defensive gunfire and the real mechanic in the crew hid in fear, Edmond fashioned a new fuel line. As he worked, enemy fire sprayed the plane and hit Edmond in the shoulder. He fell back, surrendering to despair. He withdrew a small black-and-white picture of the film's heroine from his breast pocket—an image that looked remarkably like the one of Elodie that Benjamin had lost. The sight of his dame was enough to spur him on so he could finish repairing the bomber.

Benjamin gritted his teeth. It was no wonder the studio made him sign a non-disclosure agreement about the events of the war. They'd been using him to get material for a film. Ben leaned forward in his seat to see Clyde's face cast with light from the screen. The man stared straight ahead, too low to see the rubbish spanning wall to wall in front of them. His gaze flitted to Ben's then fell even lower to where he wrung his hands in his lap.

The ignition of the bomber's engine drew Ben's focus back to the film. When the pilot slumped in his seat, succumbing to his bullet wounds, Clyde's character took the helm. Amidst enemy fire, he taxied the plane down a makeshift runway and lifted his crew out of danger and into freedom. The cheers from the audience cut straight through Ben.

To think he'd once called Clyde his friend. Nausea wrenched his stomach. His hand felt slick where he held Elodie's. She was no longer watching the movie. One hundred percent of her attention fell on Ben.

He was ruining this for her. The screen's light faded as Edmond pondered the reality of war. Ben used the cover of darkness as he sought the exit door to the right of the screen. On the other side, the hall was barely lit, perfect for sinking into his shadowed thoughts. He heard voices. No, this wasn't quite private enough. A velvet curtain blocked a doorway on his left. Ben ducked inside, where a few steps led up onto the stage. From behind the screen, Ben watched Edmond reunite with Marguerite. Clyde got the girl again.

A hand touched Ben's arm. He jerked back.

Elodie, in her delicate satin dress, looked elegant and classy. "I'm right here, Benjamin. Talk to me."

A few yards away, the film played on the back side of the screen. The soldiers were welcomed home with a grand parade. Edmond stood in the center with Marguerite at his side as he addressed the crowd, thanking them for their support on the home front.

"That was your story. You were the one who took the bullet, fixed the fuel line, and saved that flight crew. Did you fly the plane too?"

"No. When Mickey, our pilot, got shot, the co-pilot took over, but I took over his duties. It was a team effort to get home." All except Clyde, who'd hidden in the plane the entire time. They'd never have been in that mess if it weren't for him. Fortunately, they'd all escaped with their lives and a command to remain tight-lipped—for the sake of morale, they were told.

It was all clear now. Clyde Irving's fledgling career was riding on his war-time heroics.

"When I got the order to keep him alive, I knew my strengths would go to waste. I didn't think I was providing him and the filmmakers with material. That scene in the church, those were my cries, my prayers. We'd just come upon a ghastly sight, and I'd sought the Lord's presence in the church. I opened my Bible to Psalms, where I kept your picture. You were gone. I searched my bag, but it was nowhere to be found. Just that day, we'd received news about the worsening conditions of Santo Tomas. It was too much. And Clyde—my friend—used that."

The film's final scene culminated in a musical crescendo. The credits began with the first image displaying Clyde Irving's name. The writing was mirror-imaged, but it was easy to decipher: *Based on the true heroic acts of Captain Clyde Irving.* The audience cheered for each of the big names. There was no mention of Mickey or the others who'd risked their lives so the filmmakers could get their footage. Certainly no mention of Ben.

And after all the conversations he and Clyde had shared. It had been Clyde who'd helped him find the bronze angel in the rubble of the church—a part of a wall sconce that had been broken in pieces by the bomb blast. It was that small, palm-sized angel that Ben had carried around for the remaining few months of his time in Europe. The one he held whenever he longed to remember Elodie's kind heart, good soul, and loving ways—all the good he'd enlisted to protect.

"And then he came here to woo you, knowing good and well how I feel about you."

The golden hue of the credits set Elodie's face aglow as she inched closer. "How do you feel about me?"

How many times had he held back his feelings because of timing, school, war, or most recently, her health? But more than that, she'd never seemed ready to hear it. Things had changed this past month, though. And the hunger in her eyes was nearly enough to make his knees buckle.

As if to urge him on, she hesitantly slid her gloved hand over his scarred shoulder to his neck. The gentle touch roused enough courage to finally unlock the caged words he'd so long wanted to say.

"I love you, El."

She stilled a long moment, but then, a coy smile arose. "Why haven't you said anything to me before?"

"Because I never imagined you might feel the same."

Her hand on his neck guided him toward her. The fingers of her other hand pinched the lapel of his suit jacket, tugging him closer until no space remained. Her breath teased him. "And what if I do?"

"Then, I'd say we have a lot to figure out," he whispered.

The moment her lips brushed his, the loudest orchestra in the world couldn't have drowned out the pounding in his chest. He slid his hands around her waist, taking in the silky feel of her. She melted into his embrace, tilting her head back to welcome the full breadth of his kiss.

He slipped his hand beneath the curls on her neck. It didn't seem real, sharing this intimate moment with her. After imagining it countless times, her mouth was warmer, her lips smoother, and her hair softer. There weren't enough prayers in his heart to show his thankfulness.

Chapter Ten

E lodie held her hands over Ben's eyes as they walked into the hangar. She knew him. He'd sneak a peek if she just told him to close his eyes. He got too excited around surprises.

"This better be worth me nearly breaking my neck," he said.

"It's worth it."

"I hope it involves a kiss."

"Only if you're good." Elodie bit at the grin taking over her face. What kind of dream had she stumbled into, where Benjamin Gabriel desired to kiss her? She took in a deep breath. "Almost there. And stop." She didn't drop her hands quite yet. He was warm despite the frigid prairie air they'd just escaped. And he smelled like cinnamon. Like home. After all, he'd spent the morning baking cinnamon-swirl bread with her mother for tonight's dance. She stood behind him, resting her cheek on his shoulder. Still unbelievable. This was Benjamin, her friend. And now, much more.

She had no idea how he might react when he saw her surprise. Hopefully, he'd appreciate it, but as she could attest, not all wartime reminders were welcome. "Three, two, one." She dropped her hands and stepped to the side to gauge his response.

When Benjamin saw the B-24J Liberator, he inhaled sharply. "Is this. . .? It is. The *Elmira Jane*. I was wondering why you wanted to leave a big empty spot on the floor."

"I had it flown in for the occasion. I hope you don't mind."

"I think it's great." Like he had a dozen or so times since they'd first kissed last night, Benjamin took her in his arms and held her tight against him.

She allowed herself to soak in his tenderness and warmth. Her Benjamin. After a few moments, she skimmed her lips over his earlobe. "Will you show it to me?"

"Absolutely." He led her to the side of the plane, where he explained the origin of the name and all about the crew assigned to it.

But as he spoke, Elodie could only focus on the bullet holes dotting the fuselage. Ben caught her concern, stopping his story about an Oklahoman named Rip, who was a gunner. He kissed her forehead. "It's okay. We all survived."

Barely. He found a ladder and opened up the panel concealing the engine they'd lost. This engine had since been entirely replaced, but Benjamin explained the mechanics of the trauma inflicted by the anti-aircraft flak. Flying with only three engines was difficult but not impossible for a B-24. But the flak also severed the main fuel lines leading to one of the remaining engines. Benjamin described how he finagled a temporary fix to get them back up in the air. According to him, the *Elmira Jane* flew five more missions in late 1944 and early 1945. None of those missions were as problematic as the one with Clyde and Benjamin, though.

An hour later, the two sat in the back of the plane, enjoying their newfound closeness. She dragged her fingertip along his jawline, hinge to chin. His lips, full and soft, contrasted quite nicely to the slight scratch of his skin. Each time he smiled, it only enticed her to kiss him again. Would she ever tire of it? Unlikely. She'd kiss him forever and a day.

If only things were different. . .

"Eight days. That's all the time we have left together."

Benjamin said nothing. He merely dipped his chin.

"Are you sure you have to leave? Japan is so far away."

"You know how the Army works. Still, it's going to be a tough good-bye." He squeezed her tighter to himself.

"Let's not think about it, okay? We have a big night. Can you believe we're pulling this off?"

"I knew you could do it. When you put your mind to something, whether it's nursing soldiers back to health or throwing a spectacular fundraiser to help those soldiers and their families, you do it. I couldn't be more proud of you. I know your family and this community feel the same way. We are so fortunate to know you, Lieutenant Elodie Wise."

When tears blurred her vision, she buried her face against his collar. She'd always loved him as her friend. But that love had transcended to new heights in the last few weeks.

"I know you'll be busy with your hosting duties tonight, and I'll be busy making sure everything runs smoothly behind the scenes, but remember, you promised me a dance."

She looked up. "I wouldn't miss the chance." She welcomed his next string of kisses until he mumbled something against her neck.

"What did you say?" she asked.

His eyes lifted to hers, and his thumb caressed her cheek. "*Mon ange.*"

Her thoughts flitted back to her high school French class when he'd asked her to translate those two words. Mon ange. . .my angel.

Chapter Eleven

"Ben, Mrs. Handel brought all kinds of delicacies from her bakery. Where should she set them?" Mrs. Wise positively beamed as she held a platter of croissants and scones next to his landlady.

"Those look delicious, Mrs. Handel. Thank you for the donation. All the food will be set on that table back there by the bomber." Ben motioned to the long table they'd borrowed from the local art gallery. Food had started piling up, thanks to the generosity of the town. From the looks of it, folks had saved up their rations for a celebration such as this. Everything had come together perfectly. Soon, guests would start arriving, and the festivities would begin. Last he heard, the three men Elodie had hoped to honor tonight had boarded a bus in San Francisco and were en route to Hope Hill. If all went well, they'd arrived at the hangar around nine p.m.

Ben had a great feeling about all the good that would come from this event. Yet, he was most excited to see his girl and finally continue that dance from more than four years ago. His thoughts drifted to the way it felt to hold Elodie in his arms.

"Ben?" A most unwelcome voice clamored over his memory of her kisses.

Clyde Irving sported a much more elegant suit than Benjamin's. His hair had been expertly slicked back, and his mustache was trimmed and oiled. All in all, he looked slimier than Ben had ever seen him. Close behind him, Richard followed.

Ben tried for a greeting but found none to suffice.

"Looking sharp, brother," Clyde said, dusting Ben's shoulder.

Brother. What a term. He knocked Clyde's hand away.

The smarmy smile disappeared from Clyde's face. "I wanted to speak with you before everything gets started. About the movie."

Ben didn't try to hide his disgust. It was undoubtedly written all over his face. When Clyde saw it, he retreated a step. "I hope you enjoyed it, and it didn't bring back too many terrible memories."

The scoff burst from Ben's throat before he could trap it. "Oh, it brought back memories. But I remember things a bit differently than you. 'Based on the true heroic acts of Clyde Irving,' isn't that what it said? This was never about serving the country, was it? It was all about image. You were foolhardy before the war, but rather than letting the horrors of what we witnessed change you for the better, you held tight to your reckless behavior."

Clyde bristled under the barrage.

"You know, when I was first assigned to be your guardian, I was angry. What sense did it make to take a good mechanic and sock him with babysitting duties when he could have been making a real difference in the fight? But in time, I got to know you. I considered you a friend, and I would've been honored to risk my life to save yours. So this is a bit of a sucker-punch for me. I was a pawn, wasn't I?"

"No. Ben, I don't have a lot of close friends. You're one of the few—"

"Is Elodie part of your plan too? She is, isn't she? It was you and your team that leaked those stories about the two of you being a couple. You don't care about her or Heroes of Hope Hill. You only care about cleaning up your image so you can sell more movie tickets."

"Ben—"

All the heat building within Ben seemed to center beneath his ever-tightening collar. He pinned Clyde with a glare. What possible excuse would the man give now?

"I need to get ready for my hosting duties. Excuse me." Clyde walked toward the stage where the swing band was warming up with their instruments.

The anger within Ben threatened to consume him. He focused his sights on the angel topping the Christmas tree at the center of the stage. He'd told Elodie to take her time getting ready. He'd handled all the prep work. But he needed to see her right about now.

A brisk draft tickled his cheek, and he turned toward the door. Elodie seemed to glide in on the wintry breeze. Her father welcomed her, helping her slide out of her coat.

Everything else in the hangar faded out of focus. All he could see was her in that candy-apple red dress. It wrapped her waist in folds of fabric then splayed out in a full skirt that showed off her lengthy gams. Urging his eyes back to the prettiest of all faces, he couldn't remember what it had been like to not long to kiss her. Her glossy lips formed a heart-of-a-smile in his direction. Probably due to the way he was gawking at her beauty. He wanted to welcome her, but he didn't remember how to walk.

Instead, she came to him, sauntering the whole way, as if to tease him even more. "Aren't you handsome all dressed up?"

"And you. . .you are too heavenly for this world."

She curtsied. "Why, thank you." She kissed his cheek, then laughed. "I think I've staked my claim on you with lipstick." She rubbed at his cheek with her thumb. "Is everything ready?"

"Yes, we are. Are you nervous?"

"No. All I have to do is tell people about the good this charity does. Nothing I add will be more powerful than that. And afterward, you'll be the one walking me to my door and kissing me good night. If everything falls apart, at least I'll have that."

The hangar thudded with the beat as the band played "Chattanooga Choo Choo." The familiar lyrics tickled Elodie's funny bone, especially when she met Benjamin's gaze through the crowd. Joy threatened to burst forth from her in a lindy-hop, but she settled for tapping the toe of her sling-back against the floor until she finished her conversation.

"As I was saying, we'd love to bring on a medical professional such as yourself to help with the veterans at our clinic," Dr. Carol Phelps said. As a board member for Heroes of Hope Hill and a notable name in the area of psychology, she was someone Elodie had long admired. "We're funding research into the treatment of flak happiness. You know, shell shock."

Elodie's heart swelled. "What important work. Your early research on the effects of trauma on the brain has helped many people. I've seen how flashbacks following stressful events, especially battle, can be debilitating. I'd be honored to play a part. Where is your clinic?"

"We'd like to open one right here in Hope Hill. With the proximity to Kansas City, we can serve many returning soldiers." The doctor patted Elodie's hand. "Let's stay in touch. Great work tonight. No matter how much money is raised, you've brought much-needed awareness to our cause."

As Dr. Phelps breezed through the crowd, gentle hands settled on Elodie's shoulders.

"Is it time for our dance yet?" Benjamin cooed in her ear.

She leaned back against his chest. The gossip hounds in town might get enough fodder for a week, but Elodie didn't care. With their time together ticking down, she wouldn't miss a moment of affection over the fear of what others might say was appropriate. Elodie guessed he felt similarly considering how he pecked her cheek.

A dozen yards away, Richard spat words at Clyde and poked a finger into his chest. Clyde shook his lowered head but didn't look up at the man. Elodie had managed to avoid Clyde all night. After what she had seen in the film and learned from Benjamin, she no longer admired the man behind the handsome face. She was thankful for the crowd he'd attracted to the dance, but she'd be just as happy to bid him farewell.

"What do you think? Trouble in paradise?" she asked.

"Knowing Clyde, I'm sure there's something in the works. Let's not let him ruin our dance." Benjamin stepped around her. He took her left hand in his and circled his arm around her waist.

Over Benjamin's shoulder, she caught Clyde's eye. He skulked over to the two of them. "Elodie, I need to speak to you."

Before Elodie could voice her refusal, Benjamin turned sharply to Clyde. "Do you mind? I want one dance with her."

"It's important. It might change some things."

Benjamin stiffened. He clenched his fists, and Elodie tensed. Benjamin Gabriel wasn't one to make a scene, but Clyde's antics might have pushed him too far. Fortunately, her father appeared in the nick of time. He glanced curiously between the two men, then at Elodie.

"Sweetheart, there's a telegram—from George." He held out the paper. "It isn't good."

She snatched it, then thought better of the action. "Sorry. Thank you, Daddy." As quick as she could, she skimmed the words, pressing a hand to her heart as if to keep it from thudding to the floor. She placed the telegram in Benjamin's hand.

With Clyde peering over his shoulder, he read the bad news silently to himself.

"I guess I should make an announcement."

"Good idea." Her father blew out a breath. "I'll find Mrs. Weston."

"And I'll see to Rhoda," Benjamin said.

Clyde grabbed Elodie's arm. "When you're done, come find me outside. Out the back door."

"All right." As Elodie took to the stage, Benjamin moved between the dancing couples to where Rhoda was sipping punch.

As the song concluded, the band leader stepped back from the microphone and waved his hand to welcome Elodie to it.

She mouthed a thank-you, then positioned herself to speak to the more than three hundred attendees. "I'd like to thank all of you for this united effort to raise support for Heroes of Hope Hill. Clyde and I are both honored to thank our soldiers and welcome them home. However, we've just received a telegram from our local son, George Weston. He, Willis Cathy, and Eugene Rosenthal were able to board a bus in San Francisco. But this morning, the bus broke down on the Colorado and Wyoming state line. Unfortunately, they won't be able to make it home tonight."

A lament rippled through the crowd. Locals and celebrities alike covered their mouths. When Rhoda's shoulders rolled forward, Benjamin held her, then nodded at Elodie. What a great man he was. For the thousandth time, she cursed his transfer. If only there were something to be done. Some reason for him to stay here that would still allow him to use his talents for good. *Please, Lord.*

"May we all pray that they make it home for Christmas Day. When they do, your generous donations will be here waiting for them." She left the stage to the band and hurried down the steps.

Clyde was nowhere to be found. Must already be out back waiting for her with whatever gobbledygook he had to say. Chatter and a new song filled the hangar as Elodie made her way toward the back door.

Her mother appeared, her face beaming when she found Elodie. "Dear, you need to come with me. There's someone you must talk to." With hands on Elodie's shoulders, she gently steered Elodie back into the gathering of people.

"Sorry, Mama, I'm supposed to meet with Clyde. He says it's important."

"I don't believe anything he says could be more important than this. Trust me."

Chapter Twelve

Once Ben had convinced Rhoda that the sky hadn't fallen, and George would indeed be home soon, he left her to rejoin her girlfriends. If anyone knew the pain of having a love miles away, it was Ben. The back door of the hangar where Elodie was meeting with Clyde was only one hundred feet from where he stood, and Ben couldn't wait to get to her side. How much farther was Japan than that? It had been hard enough during the war, but now that he knew how good it felt to kiss her, hold her, and tell her he loved her?

The tension in his shoulders pulled his scar tissue taut, and he scratched at it. If only he'd trusted God with his future, his worth, his identity, he wouldn't have looked for one more way to prove himself and volunteered for this next assignment a world away.

He headed toward the door, bypassing the *Elmira Jane* and the guests examining the bullet holes in the side. When he opened the hangar's back door, a welcome gust rushed into the space. The heaters hadn't been necessary after all the folks had begun dancing.

Outside, the night offered a peaceful contrast to the soaring noise of the dance. While he'd expected to hear Clyde's camera-ready voice spinning some tale for Elodie, the only sounds were the whooshing grasses of a moonlight-tinged field. Where had the two of them gone?

Thud.

It sounded like something had bumped against the hangar's wall, but there was nothing out here. He crept to the corner and peeked around.

The tall form of a man stood against the hangar's steel side, where even the moonlight couldn't reach. He was facing away from Benjamin and dredged in shadow, but his broad shoulders and slick, dark hair erased all mystery. Clyde.

Ben's fists clenched. Finally, he could tell the guy just what he thought about his stunts over the past two and a half years. He opened his mouth to call out his former friend's name but paused when a woman's hand curled around Clyde's upper arm. More than the December air, the sound of kisses sent a chill into the marrow of Ben's bones.

Clyde shuffled his feet.

Thud, thud.

A golden blond curl fell over Clyde's shoulder as he and Elodie giggled together. Nausea arrested Ben's stomach, and when the two resumed their kissing, Ben backed away, nearly tripping on a rock.

Elodie was merely confused. In just a few weeks, Ben had pushed her from friendship to well, what was it? They hadn't defined it yet. What point was there in going steady or courting when Ben was leaving in a little over a week? It had been an emotional night following a hard few years. And Clyde Irving was Clyde Irving after all. He shouldn't blame her.

He could forgive a few stolen kisses, couldn't he? They would talk about it and figure out what their future might hold.

Still, anger raced through his veins, and he cursed it. If he had one of Elodie's syringes, he'd bleed himself dry if it meant being rid of any malice toward her.

A lanky man with thinning auburn hair turned toward Elodie and her mother, greeting them with a smile. "Lieutenant Wise. Woman of the hour."

"Elodie, this is Colonel J.P. Chesterton. Your father and I have known him for a long time," her mother said.

He held out his hand. Though a bit more aged, the skin was stained with the same grease that marked Benjamin's calloused palms. "Sorry about that. These mechanic mitts always give me away before I can introduce myself." He recoiled his hand, but Elodie grasped it, shaking it firmly.

"A colonel with grease on his hands?" Elodie raised a brow. Normally, she wouldn't speak to a superior with such informality, but it was a night of goodwill and celebration, and Colonel Chesterton had a gracious way about him.

"I work for the War Department, specifically in the area of aircraft procurement. I was up at Fairfax Field earlier today checking the quality of the remaining C-47s before they head to Topeka. Can't let the young ones have all the fun, can I?"

Elodie grinned.

Her mother pressed her hands together in front of her waist. "While he won't tell me specifically what special projects they have going—"

"It's confidential. You understand," Colonel Chesterton explained.

Her mother continued. "He said he's heard about how skilled Benjamin is."

Elodie nodded. "Oh, yes. Benjamin's a genius when it comes to engines. Cars, trains, and aircraft, especially."

"As you know, threats still abound in the world, and we're always looking to create the strongest aircraft for our boys. We're looking at some contracts with outside companies to develop new aviation technology, and I'd love to have Benjamin's knowledge and experience."

Hope flitted inside Elodie. "I'm sorry to tell you, sir, that Benjamin is one of the replacement troops being sent to occupy Japan just after the first of the year."

"Well, that won't do. If he doesn't mind staying closer to home, I believe his skills would be put to better use here in the U.S. I can move some chess pieces on my end to make that happen. Is there anything you could do to convince him to stick around Missouri?"

The warmth of a hundred Filipino summers flooded Elodie. Her happily ever after was so close, she could kiss it. "I'm sure I could think of something."

Elodie's mother tilted her head as if to say *I told you so*.

Perhaps her hovering ways weren't so terrible after all.

"Now, ladies and gentlemen, the band has a special Christmas treat for us," Clyde said from the stage. Whatever had been bothering him, he must've forgotten about it, for he was sure beaming now. "And if you don't mind, I'd like to welcome to the stage, my cohost, Lieutenant Elodie Wise, for a dance."

Elodie shook her head, but the crowd's applause urged her forward. She climbed the stage with hesitation. He was not the man she wished to dance with tonight. Especially not now. She longed to find Benjamin and tell him about Colonel Chesterton's job offer. She scanned the audience—no Benjamin. As the band began to play "Have Yourself a Merry Little Christmas," she accepted Clyde's hand, though she reserved her smile.

"Why so glum? This is going well."

"I'm not glum. Tonight *is* going well. But it would be better if the soldiers were home. And if the right people were getting the glory."

His brow wrinkled. "I saw you go after Ben during the final part of the movie last night. He was pretty upset, wasn't he?"

"Yes. He's an honorable man with the heart of a hero. It's a shame he wasn't able to prove that to the world." What was on his lips? They were tinged pink.

"Yes. A shame to be sure." He clamped his lips together. "You really like him, don't you?"

"Yes, Clyde. I love him."

"Excuse me, folks." Richard's voice in the microphone brought the band's music to a dissonant halt. "I hate to interrupt this great music, but while we have our two hosts up here together, this appears to be the best time to make an exciting announcement. If you think these two lovebirds look good together on stage, just you wait."

"Do you know anything about this?" Elodie whispered.

Clyde leaned in. "This is what I was trying to warn you about."

Richard motioned to two of his crewmembers. They pulled strings connected to something Elodie hadn't seen earlier. A stage-wide roll of paper had been tacked to the wall behind the Christmas tree. When the roll released, it displayed a poster with both Clyde and Elodie's pictures. In big block letters, it read The Irving-Wise Tour. Below that, in smaller print, it promised visits to "a town near you."

Elodie dropped her hands to her sides.

"That's right. These lovebirds are hitting the rails on a fifteen-city tour to raise money for our brave soldiers returning to the home front. The first stop is on December 27 in Birmingham."

Lovebirds? No. This was all wrong. The walls of the hangar swayed like the trees in the jungle. Elodie needed to settle her breathing, or she wouldn't be able to think.

"Elodie?" Clyde was too close. He looked pale, but perhaps that was her vision succumbing to the headache.

"I never agreed to this, Clyde."

"Elodie, I'll make this right. I promise."

"Now back to the music," the bandleader said. "How about some "Jingle Bells"?

Elodie backed away from Clyde and nearly stumbled down the steps of the stage. Benjamin. He needed to know this was not her doing. But where had he gone? Above everyone's heads, she saw the exit door swing closed. She pushed her way through the dancing couples.

Patricia Ridgeway tugged Elodie's hand. "Congratulations on the tour. Like I was saying last night, I hope to play you in a movie." She twirled a barrel curl around her finger. "I've already got the hair for it."

"I'm sorry, but I must go." Elodie withdrew her hand, but by the time she pushed her way through the door and out into the crammed parking lot, all she saw was taillights.

Chapter Thirteen

B en sat outside the Wises' dark home in his truck. In his hands, he held a box big enough to hold his heart, but not all the emotions he felt for Elodie. The thin wrapping had torn at the corners from too much handling and fretting. He'd already held on to it too long. He may as well give it to her. And maybe that way, he could let her go.

Where had he gotten things so wrong? Why had she allowed Clyde to kiss her? And why had she agreed to go on this tour without telling him? His brain hurt trying to process it all. That was the problem. He loved her too much to see things as they were.

He dropped the small box onto the stack of presents he'd brought for the members of the Wise family. Beneath Elodie's, he saw Rhoda's name on the tag. What was Elodie's philosophy when she felt troubled or scared? Look for someone to help. That he could do. But it would take time and space, which was exactly what he needed right now.

Elodie stepped into her home as the clock struck midnight. Was this how Cinderella felt in that old story by the Brothers Grimm? Her time of festivities was over. Now she must return to her ordinary life, but in this version, it was she who was searching for her prince. No golden slipper in sight.

Only a dim light filtered down the hall—from the Christmas tree most likely. Still, her home lacked its usual warmth, and she kept her coat on to fight off the chill pressing against her bones. She made her way into the family room.

Her mother sat in her rocking chair with a cup of tea in her hand. "Any luck?"

Elodie slumped on the couch. "I can't find him anywhere. No one in town has seen him since the dance."

"Give him time, sweetheart. The two of you have made it through far worse things than this."

Elodie swallowed against the lump in her throat that might never dissolve. "We didn't even get our dance."

"Have faith. Hope is never lost when you have faith." Her mother sipped her tea. "I can't tell you how often I reminded myself of that very thing while you were gone. And here you are—still my courageous girl, helping others at every opportunity."

"You and Daddy taught me well. I never agreed to this publicity tour. If Benjamin thought I did, it would break his heart. He'll think I chose to spend his last week with Clyde rather than him. No wonder he left."

"Wherever he went, he stopped by here first."

Elodie angled to face her mother. "How do you know that?"

"Look under the tree."

Elodie kneeled at the foot of the fir she and Benjamin had purchased at the tree lot. Her heart panged at the sweet memory of strolling down Main Street with him, making sledding plans that would never come to pass.

A stack of gifts rested on top of the tree skirt. A joint present for her parents, one for Charlie, one for Rhoda, and finally a small one for her. All from Benjamin. On hers, beneath his name, it said Open immediately.

"I'll let you be alone. Would you like a lamp on?"

"No. I prefer the dark. Thank you."

Elodie waited for her mother to leave the room, then untied the ribbon, letting it fall to her lap. She slipped her nail beneath the seam, loosening the tape. Once the paper had been removed, all that remained was a simple white box. She lifted the lid carefully. Inside, on a pillow of tissue paper, a bronze cherub greeted her. She lifted it out and held it, taking in the intricate curves of its wings. A small slip of paper stuck to the inside of the box. She unfolded it and read his words to her.

Mon ange,

There was a time in France when everything I understood about the world was turned upside down and covered in rubble. What good could exist in a world so overcome with evil? It was the question that led to my wrestling with God in that church. That was when I found this angel. I believe it had once been part of a sconce. When I saw it, I thought of you and the others in this world that seek to do good in the hardest of circumstances. I carried this with me in my pack for the remainder of my time. In the absence of your picture, this is what I held to think of you. I thought you might like to add it to your nativity set to replace the one I broke years ago.

Love to you always,

Benjamin

A tear dropped onto the note. Elodie wiped her cheeks on the sleeve of her coat. She stood, carrying the angel and the note to the mantel where the crèche sat. Inside, the Holy Family were flanked by the three wise men and the shepherd. Elodie carefully placed the angel behind the manger to watch over the infant Jesus.

She backed away and pressed the note to her chest. *Oh Benjamin, where are you?*

Chapter Fourteen

The day before Christmas crawled by. Elodie drove to Benjamin's home several times, but he still hadn't returned. Mama made supper, but Elodie couldn't find the appetite to eat. Neither could Clyde, it seemed. She didn't like having him across the table from her, but Daddy forbade her from sending him packing when they'd promised him a place to stay for the holiday.

Elodie stared hard at the man who wouldn't meet her eye until Charlie kicked her shin. "Ouch! What was that for?"

Charlie said nothing, just scooped a bite of pickled herring into her mouth. Nasty stuff.

At Elodie's side, Benjamin's seat remained empty. They'd all hoped he'd be back by now. After dinner, while the family settled in to listen to carols on the radio, Elodie excused herself to bed. She stared at the ceiling, praying for Benjamin wherever he might be.

As a girl, she'd listened for St. Nicholas's sleigh bells on Christmas Eve, but now she listened for any sign that her love had returned to her. Around eleven, a scuffle sounded from the side yard beneath Elodie's bedroom window. She bolted upright, listening. A muffled man's voice rose from below.

Elodie threw on her robe and hurried out of her room, padding past Mama and Daddy's door and down the stairs. She left the house through the back door. If it was Benjamin, she didn't want her family waking up to witness their reunion.

A few light snowflakes drifted lazily past her nose. All was calm this Christmas Eve. No more scuffling.

"Benjamin?" she whispered into the night.

There was movement by the garage. Someone was hiding in the shadows.

Elodie took a few steps forward.

A man coughed.

"It's me." Charlie wore the dark quilt from the family room over her shoulders like a cape.

"Charlie. What on earth are you doing out here in the cold this late? Are you alone?"

"Yes," she stammered.

There was more noise from the shadows. Clyde Irving leaped into the yard, brushing the top of his hair.

Elodie squinted. "Clyde?"

"I thought a bat landed on me." After realizing he was safe from the invisible creature, he fixed his eyes on Elodie. The same sheepish expression slid over his face as her sister.

"What are you two. . .? Oh!"

Upon closer inspection, Clyde had lipstick smeared over his mouth. Elodie didn't know if she should laugh at them or scold them.

"Um, I should head to bed. Good night, Hollywood," Charlie said.

"Good night, Charlie."

Charlie pressed past Elodie, raising a brow and challenging her to say something in the process. But Elodie kept her mouth closed. Charlie wasn't one to take a reprimand lightly, especially after a long day. Elodie let the door shut behind her before looking back to Clyde.

"Sorry to interrupt," Elodie said. "I thought you might have been—"

"Ben?"

"Yes. Clearly, I was mistaken." Without a good night, she spun on her slippered heels and went inside the kitchen.

Clyde, however, followed. "Elodie, wait. We need to talk."

"I don't want—"

"Please? I need to apologize, and that isn't something I have a good deal of experience with."

Elodie groaned softly. She grabbed the bottle of milk from the fridge and a saucepan. Perhaps some warm milk would help her sleep. For once, she wanted Clyde to share one of his dull stories about life in Hollywood. That would put her out like a light.

"I had nothing to do with the tour. I've already told Richard you aren't going."

Elodie lit the burner and stared hard at the milk, willing it to warm quickly. She grabbed a wooden spoon and swirled it around the pot.

"I fired him. I'll be looking for new management in January."

Elodie stopped stirring.

"I don't like the direction my career has taken over the last few years under his guidance. I knew he was the one fueling the headlines about you and me. I didn't stop him though. I'd gotten myself in trouble in California, and I thought being tied to you might help my reputation recover. Last night, when I was waiting for you, so I could warn you about the tour announcement, your sister followed me out of the hangar. She gave me a grand lecture on learning to speak for myself."

Elodie swiveled to face him. Those ridiculous lips were stained pink like last night—

proof Charlie had given him a lesson on more than merely being spineless.

"I shouldn't have used you like that. Or Ben. The events in *Enemy Skies* were based on his heroic acts. Not mine. He took the bullet, fixed the plane. In reality, I was the reason we were behind enemy lines in the first place. When the camera was filming me in the cockpit, I steered us in the opposite direction than the pilot instructed. It was my fault we were hit by flak. I almost took Ben's life, and he responded by saving mine. He's the hero."

"I appreciate you saying that. Now, if Benjamin ever returns, will you say it to him?"

"Yes."

"And will you come clean to the papers about it?"

"Absolutely. No more lying." He scratched his cheek. "But there's more." He reached into his breast pocket. He took out a small rectangular paper, looked at it for a long moment, then with a sigh, he slid it across the counter.

The black-and-white photograph featured Elodie smiling and looking off at an angle. Her parents had arranged it for her college graduation. The edges of the picture had frayed. Part of it had faded, and there was a crease across her arm.

She picked it up, holding it gingerly, as if too firm a grip might harm the wide-eyed, naïve girl in the shot. "My photograph?"

"This was the one Ben carried in his Bible."

On her right, the milk bubbled up and over the side of the saucepan. She grabbed a towel, pulled the pan off the burner, and then switched off the flame. The burnt smell wafted past her nose, and she felt ill. "The one he lost?"

"Yeah. But he didn't lose it. I took it one night when he was sleeping."

Elodie pinched the collar of her robe together at her neck. A throb drummed her temple. "Why would you do such a thing?"

"I was jealous. I was jealous of the way he thought of you. I had no one in my past, present, or future to give me peace. I wanted you for myself. Even if it was just your picture and the childish stories he'd told."

"Why would you rob him of that?"

"Why have I done anything? I've been a selfish fool, and I'm sorry." Clyde fought to clear his throat. "He does love you, you know. It's clearer to me than the sky over the Pacific Ocean."

Chapter Fifteen

With the light streaming past the curtains, Elodie rolled to her side and bumped into a warm body in her bed.

Rhoda's wild hair fell across her face. For a moment, she looked like the fourteen-year-old Elodie had once left behind in favor of excitement and adventure. When had she slipped beneath Elodie's covers? No matter. Elodie's heart swelled seeing her baby sister do something other than pout or roll her eyes in her presence. She almost didn't want to wake her.

But she could smell bacon. Mama's Christmas morning breakfast was worth a few extra sneers from Rhoda. Elodie brushed her sister's hair off her face. On the pillowcase, beneath Rhoda's eye, a faint stain was circled in salty white. "Rhoda," she breathed.

When Rhoda awakened, she seemed as confused as Elodie over her bedfellow. Then, after a moment, tears came.

"Oh, Rhoda. What's wrong?"

"I've just missed you."

"Oh, honey." Elodie nestled Rhoda close. "I've missed you too."

"And I'm sorry I've been such a brat. I was mad that you left me. And then even when you came home, you weren't here. Not really. Your mind was still over there in the Pacific. I needed my big sister."

"I know. I'm sorry." Elodie stroked Rhoda's face gently. "At least you had Charlie."

Rhoda snorted, which sent Elodie into a fit of giggles. *Just wait until Rhoda finds out about Charlie and Clyde.*

"Still no word from Ben?"

Elodie rubbed the sleep from her eyes. "No. Have you heard from George?"

"No. Bing Crosby just keeps dashing my hopes with that "I'll Be Home for Christmas" song."

"We'll keep praying. Merry Christmas, Rhoda."

"Merry Christmas, Sis."

A heavy knock from downstairs made them both tense up. They held eye contact and their breath.

"Rhoda! Someone's here to see you," Mama called.

Rhoda's eyes rounded, and she pulled her lower lip into her mouth.

"Go on," Elodie said.

Rhoda hopped out of Elodie's bed, nearly catching her foot on the sheets. She grabbed Elodie's robe and swung it over her.

"Hey, that's my—"

And Rhoda was gone.

Elodie smiled and swung her legs off the side of her bed. She dressed quickly, craving that bacon. She might eat the whole platter now that she had her appetite back. She brushed her teeth and ran a comb through her hair, but the makeup could wait until church.

She headed down the stairs. A glance into the den showed that yes, indeed, George Weston had made it home—or at least into Rhoda's arms—for Christmas. Elodie gave George a small wave, then proceeded into the family room, allowing them their privacy. She'd known Rhoda's crush on Benjamin wasn't something to fret over.

She gathered a deep breath. If only the promise of Christmas morning presents could soothe the ache she felt in—

"Benjamin!"

He was there. Sure as Christmas morning, he was there, with one elbow leaning on the mantel by the nativity set. When he laid eyes on her, he straightened up, and his apology was written all over his face. Although she wanted more than anything to run directly to his arms, she needed understanding first.

"Where did you go?"

"Wyoming."

Elodie gasped. "You brought George home!"

"After the dance, I needed some time to think. When I was dropping off your gifts, my thoughts were really muddled, so I did what you taught me. I looked for someone I could help. I was able to fix the bus's engine so the rest of the soldiers could continue on to their families. But I made George ride with me. Wasn't taking a chance on him not making it back to Rhoda."

"Why didn't you tell me?"

"I wasn't sure I'd be able to find them. The last thing I wanted to do was get Rhoda's hopes up, so I didn't leave a note. And once I got there, I tried to call, but lines were jammed with soldiers trying to get in touch with their families."

"And you love surprises," she said, rounding the rocking chair.

Ben lowered his gaze. "Not all surprises. I didn't like stumbling on you and Clyde kissing."

Elodie nearly swallowed her tongue. "I beg your pardon?"

"At the dance, when you and Clyde went out behind the hangar."

Oh! "Benjamin, that wasn't me kissing Clyde."

"Then who was it?"

Clyde strode into the family room, stopping on a dime when he spotted Benjamin. "Oh, hello, Ben."

"Clyde, give us a few minutes?"

Realization dawned on Clyde's face. "Absolutely. But first, Elodie, have you seen Charlie?"

"I don't think she's up yet," Elodie said. "I'll tell her you're waiting for her."

Clyde remained still.

"In the kitchen." Elodie nodded for him to leave.

Clyde winked. "Right. In the kitchen."

Once Clyde had left, Ben rubbed his hands down his face. "I'm a fool."

"Maybe a bit. But you're my fool." She lifted her lips into a smile and broached the space that separated them, hopefully for the last time. "I said no to the tour."

When she neared, he squared his shoulders to face her, leaning ever so slightly. Longing swirled in his eyes. "Elodie. . ."

She sprang forward into his arms, forcing him to grab the mantel to steady himself. Unable to hold back, she pressed her lips against his, releasing all the frustration of the past thirty-six hours into him. He was strong enough to bear it. They—Elodie and Benjamin—were strong enough to bear it. Like Mother said, they'd been through worse.

Her kiss softened, welcoming his tender caresses that poured over her lips like waves on the sand. The warmth inside her flamed hotter than the fire in the hearth. She pulled away slightly, and he touched his forehead to hers.

A grimace bent his features. "I can't bear to part from you after this," he whispered.

"Funny you mention that. Do you know who Colonel J.P . Chesterton is?"

"Yeah, sure."

"He's got some top secret project he wants you to work on with him. Rumor has it, our guys are trying to produce a jet bomber to rival the Luftwaffe's. He said he could get your assignment changed *if* you had a reason to stay close."

His smile shone light straight into her darkness. It was a great smile.

"And if for some reason, they don't approve the move, I can flaunt my angel wings—that's what they're calling us now—the Angels of Bataan and Corregidor."

"That's what I heard. How did the fundraiser end up?"

"Outstanding. We more than tripled our goal, and we don't even have the final tally yet. We'll be able to help so many soldiers and families, Benjamin. And look at this." Elodie lifted her hand for him out to the side for him to see the way her fingers only quivered the slightest bit. "I don't know that I'll ever completely forget my past. Maybe I'm not supposed to, but with the Lord, my family, and you by my side, I'm no longer afraid of my future. In fact, I've been offered a job at the clinic to research how to best help those who have endured traumatic events like war."

He smiled as he took her hand in his. "Where?"

She felt heat rise to her cheeks. "Right here."

"The more I see what you're capable of, the more I'm convinced that you truly are an angel." He nodded to the nativity set. "Speaking of, do you like your gift?"

"I love it. It's the perfect addition to my family's set. One day, I look forward to passing it on to my children and my grandchildren."

"And will you tell them the story of how you got it?"

"The story of how their grandfather salvaged it from the rubble during his time in the second World War?" She twisted her lips into a playful smirk as his eyes lit up. "I won't spare a single detail."

He studied her face, pushing a curl behind her ear and letting his hand trail down the nape of her neck. "I'm not sure our grandchildren will want to know about the many kisses involved."

"Perhaps we'll keep that to ourselves."

On the way to the kitchen, they passed the window where more snowflakes flitted around.

"Too bad the snow isn't sticking," she said. "You owe me a sledding date."

Benjamin stopped and pulled her tight against him, one arm around her waist and one holding her hand against his heart. "And you owe me a dance."

"Well, you can dance with me whatever the weather for the rest of our lives. And one day, the time we've spent apart will be a mere breath compared to the years we've shared. I love you, Benjamin Gabriel."

"And I love you, mon ange."

The End

Janine Rosche is the author of *With Every Memory* and *The Road before Us*. Prone to wander, she finds as much comfort on the open road as she does at home. This longing to chase adventure, behold splendor, and experience redemption is woven into her stories. When she isn't traveling or writing novels, she teaches family life education courses, produces *The Love Wander Read Journal*, and takes too many pictures of her sleeping dogs. Visit www.JanineRosche.com for a free gift and to connect with Janine.

Dear Reader,

I truly hope you enjoyed Elodie and Benjamin's story! This one remains one of my favorites as it was inspired by my own family's heirloom nativity set. And yes, the angel was always my favorite piece! Would you consider leaving a review on Goodreads, Amazon, or Bookbub? Also, don't forget to check out The Road before Us (May 2024). Clyde and Charlie return as prominent characters in that one!

May God bless you until we meet on these pages again!

Janine Rosche